SOLD 60p

A Necessary Dealing

It began at a business function attended by Eric Ward, Newcastle solicitor and now part-time director of a London merchant bank. Eric had recently refused to represent his wealthy wife in her dealings with a Tyneside entrepreneur, but when the attractive woman chairman of a company facing a management buy-out approached him for advice, he saw no reason why he should not at least listen.

Eileen O'Hara was suspicious of the bid but her managing director and his allies had financial backing and her board were divided, not least because she was a woman. When there was a rival bid, it was left to Eric to discover that the former company secretary had met a violent end; that O'Hara and a member of her board had until recently been lovers; that the arbitrageur who now entered the lists had his own reasons for discomfiting the rival backer; in short, that all had scores to settle unconnected with the business in hand. And it was left to the police to uncover a murder, with Eric the last known person to see the victim alive.

As tension mounts in the boardroom and between Eric and his wife as she watches him drawn ever deeper into a situation that threatens both their own relationship and his position with the bank, Eric learns bitterly the kind of dealing necessary to win a boardroom battle, to save a marriage—and to uncover a murderer.

by the same author

Arnold Landon novels
THE DEVIL IS DEAD
MEN OF SUBTLE CRAFT
A TROUT IN THE MILK
MOST CUNNING WORKMEN
A GATHERING OF GHOSTS

Eric Ward novels
THE SALAMANDER CHILL
PREMIUM ON DEATH
A BLURRED REALITY
ONCE DYING, TWICE DEAD
A LIMITED VISION
DWELL IN DANGER
A CERTAIN BLINDNESS

SEEK FOR JUSTICE
A RELATIVE DISTANCE
A VIOLENT DEATH
AN INEVITABLE FATALITY
AN UNCERTAIN SOUND
NOTHING BUT FOXES
A DISTANT BANNER
WITNESS MY DEATH
A PART OF VIRTUE
DOUBLE TAKE
A QUESTION OF DEGREE
OF SINGULAR PURPOSE
BLOOD MONEY
A SECRET SINGING
THE FENOKEE PROJECT
ERROR OF JUDGEMENT
A WOLF BY THE EARS
A LOVER TOO MANY

ROY LEWIS

A Necessary Dealing

An Eric Ward novel

COLLINS, 8 GRAFTON STREET, LONDON W1

William Collins Sons & Co. Ltd
London · Glasgow · Sydney · Auckland
Toronto · Johannesburg

First published 1989
© Roy Lewis 1989

British Library Cataloguing in Publication Data

Lewis, J. R.
   A necessary dealing.—(Crime Club)
   I. Title
   823'.914[F]

ISBN 0 00 232274 9

Photoset in Linotron Baskerville by
Rowland Phototypesetting Ltd
Bury St Edmunds, Suffolk
Printed in Great Britain by
William Collins Sons & Co. Ltd, Glasgow

CHAPTER 1

1

The Tube train was crowded.

It was rarely he travelled by the Underground: the overcrowding at peak times and the proximity of the people thrusting into the carriage with him brought claustrophobic terrors that probably had deep psychological roots. Not that he was addicted to that kind of self-analysis: in fact, he was a straightforward man with a logical mind, and if the logic had sometimes been overturned by emotion, and even desire, that was merely a reflection of the human condition. His condition.

But he was miserable. Not just because he had been forced by necessity to travel by the Underground on this misty autumn evening. After all, he could have taken a cab ... except there had been none available when he left the office and it would have been an unnecessary expense, even though he did not lack for money. His misery lay deeper than such trivia: it was a compound of depressing events. He had a tidy, logical mind. Problems did not worry him: problems were for solutions, and his training as an accountant helped him analyse situations and reach acceptable solutions.

It was when emotions crowded in that the real difficulties arose.

The train was slowing—the inevitable grinding of brakes, the slow, shuddering stop, and the wait outside Camden Town, hot, sweaty, eyes avoiding others, the inexplicable tension that arose, the tension everyone denied but nevertheless felt at the unbidden thought of entombment deep below the surface in a train packed with people. He avoided eyes; he stared at the littered floor.

Emotions.

The logical solution was to treat them with logic, identify them, analyse them, weigh them in the balance and then determine a course of action. But should he keep the problem to himself? The first question to be answered, perhaps, but then there was the problem of trust. If he spoke to the other members of the board, identified for them the dangers he saw in the issues which were arising, issues of fidelity and probity as opposed to convenience and chicanery, and threw down the gauntlet, let them sort out the problems themselves, what would happen? The future of the company could lie with his silence, but he was not sure he could live with that silence. It was not merely that there were large issues at stake: there was also the principle of the thing. He could see the logic of the common good being served by the ends proposed; the thought that individuals might reap personal gains by those actions left sand in his mouth, nevertheless.

It was suddenly very hot in the carriage. He was sweating. He loosened the grey scarf he wore at his neck, shuffled his shoulders in the black overcoat, clutched his briefcase nervously between his knees. It had been a surprise, finding that the car wouldn't start that morning: it was only a few weeks since it had been serviced. But that was typical of garages these days: they just didn't exercise the care they used to years ago. He'd managed to get a lift to the office, and had expected one back home. Then the crisis had arisen, the phone had rung on his desk late in the afternoon, and the offer of a lift had been withdrawn, with apologies.

He had rung Cynthia then, but the car was not ready so she could not come to pick him up. In any case, what was wrong with the Tube?

There was a hissing of brakes, a grinding lurch and they were off again, at snail's pace, then gathering speed into the rushing darkness. He closed his eyes for a few seconds, opened them and looked around. No glances met his. Impersonal. Uncaring. Unaware of his conscience and his dilemma.

The lights sprang up from the darkness. They were arriving at the platform. The sign announced Camden Town. He rose, clutching his briefcase as others moved and shuffled towards the door. Then there was the inevitable brief crush as the doors opened, a crowd of humanity surging on to the platform. He hung back, reluctant to fight his way towards the stairs. Then, as the crowd thinned, he followed along behind, head down, staring at the ground, thinking.

Directors had a duty towards the company; so did employees. The same duties, in essence—of care, and fidelity.

The word clutched coldly at his chest and for a moment he was no longer thinking of the company and the issues that had been churning around in his mind for weeks, as the negotiations had got under way and he had slowly become aware of the emerging facts.

Fidelity.

Cynthia.

What did fidelity actually mean, in a marriage? There was the mind, and there was the body. A snatch of an old song came to him, unbidden, as he reached the escalator and began the ride to the surface. 'I'm always true to you, darling, in my fashion . . .'

Yet he had always thought that fidelity was a basic, clearly defined concept with a practical reality behind it, a determinant of conduct. But others would not hold the same view, of that he was aware. He was an ageing, dusty-viewed, unimaginative accountant with a wife who had been brought up in a society younger and more open than his, and he had no right to impose his attitudes upon her. Yet he hardly knew what her views were, nor what her attitudes might be.

He had never asked.

Asking could mean answers and heartbreak.

The rushing wind at the top of the stairs was cold on his face, offering him a foretaste of the dark violence of the street beyond. He handed in his ticket to the uninterested collector and passed through the gates. There was the usual scattering of meths drinkers and inebriated Irish layabouts in the station entrance: two were squabbling half-heartedly over a dark-coloured bottle. One caught his glance and broke away. He shambled forward, barring the exit.

'Gotta helpin' hand for a friend in trouble, mister?'

The Irishman saw the horror in his eyes.

'Just a cup of tea, for Chrissake!' The glazed glance of the Irishman changed, sharpening malevolently as he brushed past. 'Bastard! We'll meet again, we will!'

There was a roar of traffic in the street, the lights were changing, he crossed quickly into Parkway, anxious that the drunks should not pursue him. It was almost seven in the evening, the Parkway had seen its own rush hour and the streets were becoming quiet. He walked quickly along the uneven pavement, towards the Regent's Park.

It was not far to the flat. He had bought the first-floor property ten years ago, when Cynthia had wanted to move closer into London. It had been a good investment: it had more than quadrupled in value. Perhaps what was been worked on at the company would be a good investment, too. But there were snags, ethical issues to be faced, brought out into the open.

And only he could do it. The others were involved, they stood to gain. And he was the compliance officer for the company, after all, the company secretary, the only statutory officer in the company. If *he* did not stand firm, challenge the legality of their proposed actions, expose the conflict of interest that was arising, who else could do it?

He turned right into Prince Albert Road. The Regent's Park was on his left, the canal and dark trees muting the roar of central London and the West End beyond. He walked swiftly, his shoes making little noise. A taxi rushed past, its headlights bright in his eyes, but there was no one else walking. He kept his head down, the anxieties churning in his mind. The company . . . and Cynthia.

His faith, his Catholicism, had taught him that man and wife were one. His own needs had made him regard his wife as a confidante: they were one. But not in all things, he suspected . . . yet suspicions were unworthy, and unhealthy, and dangerous.

Cynthia.

He reached the junction near St Mark's Church. The square lay down to his right. Someone was stepping out of the side road. They were almost in collision.

He stepped aside, muttering an apology, and then a hand reached out, grabbing at his briefcase. He clung to it, terrified, feeling the bile rise in his throat and then he was swung violently sideways, crashing against the low wall. He tried to shout but the call was cut off short as the knife thudded into his chest. Partly turned aside by the thickness of his overcoat, the thrust was not lethal, but it winded him, cutting off his cry. Then the glinting blade slashed wickedly upwards, taking him just under the chin, and he felt the coldness and the warmth and the quick gush of blood. He staggered back, relinquishing his grip on the briefcase, choking as the warm salty liquid filled his mouth and throat and he fell forward on to his knees, a supplicant begging for life in the rushing darkness.

She was there, bright and sparkling as she used to be, there in his mind as he died.

2

'These occasions always remind me of the old Castilian proverb, don't you know?' Lord Evenhulme snickered, waving his glass of whisky under Eric's nose and almost spilling some of it upon Anne's grey suit. 'We have to listen to a speech that's very like the horns of a bull. You know . . . a point here . . . a point there . . . and an awful lot of bull in between!'

The septuagenarian leered at Anne who managed to offer a distantly polite smile in return. Eric looked away, seeking some means of escape from the corner in which they had been trapped by the lecherous old bore who was well enough known on the northern circuit for his own interminable speeches.

'This is the first time I've attended the Award lunch,' he heard Anne saying.

'Your company is in line for the award?'

'We've made the last six,' Anne said off-handedly, but not entirely successful in keeping the pride out of her tone. 'But the whisper is the prize has gone elsewhere.'

'Hah! Damn shame! Now if I'd had my way I'd have looked beyond the beauty of a damned piece of print . . .'

'George, old boy!'

They were saved. Major-General Percy Bedford, CB, now retired to the kind of job the City reserved affectionately for retired admirals and generals, was bearing down upon Lord Evenhulme. His glass was raised to avoid it being upset in the crush of dark-suited men thronging here in the Egyptian Room of the Mansion House. Eric took Anne by the elbow and adroitly steered her out of the path of the advancing major-general, turning her so that Evenhulme was unable to continue to hold her eye, and he moved sideways towards the waitress with the tray of charged glasses. He took an orange juice for himself, and a glass of white wine for Anne as she got rid of the empty glass she had been holding for some time, while trapped by her House of Lords admirer.

'I thought we were there for the duration.'

'Saved by a major-general.'

'An unusual experience for the troops.'

'You sound cynical enough to have served in the Army.'

'You know better. It was the boys in blue for me.'

Anne sipped her wine. 'Old Bedford's as bad as our lecherous friend Evenhulme. What *was* he in the war, anyway?'

'Director of Movements, at the War Office.'

'*Really?*' Anne managed to keep a straight face for all of five seconds and then she giggled, raising one hand over her mouth in that curiously childish gesture she had never lost, even on public occasions.

'Really, I have to admit they could have thought of a more . . . acceptable title. But maybe he actually was in charge of—'

'Eric, please! This is a serious occasion. We'll be going in shortly. I can't enter with all you sober-suited men around me and be seen all red in the face from suppressed giggles!'

Eric glanced around the crowded room. 'There are other women here; it's not all men.'

'Ninety per cent. Though I have to admit, the women who *are* here are pretty striking. If I'd known they were going to dress up . . .'

Eric looked at his wife. She appeared cool and elegant in her grey suit and white blouse, her businesslike clothing in no way detracting from either her femininity or her beauty. The red-gold tints were still in her hair as they had been the first time he saw her, riding in the Northumberland hills; her figure was more mature now, more rounded, but still well proportioned, and she carried herself well, her head up, her eyes challenging. 'I'll settle for you,' he said quietly.

She glanced at him quizzically, then looked around the room, appraising the opposition. 'Even so, there's that plump little piece over there in that black number, and that off-the-shoulder red and black in the corner . . . are you sure this is the International Stock Exchange Annual Awards lunch, and not some meeting place for businessmen and their elegant floozies?'

'I do so assure you, my dear Anne,' came a voice from behind them. 'St John's Wood was always the place for discreet town houses and assignations, and I don't believe things have changed that much. But the Mansion House ... never, I believe.'

Anne turned, and smiled warmly at the man who had spoken. 'Leonard! I hadn't realized you'd be here!'

'Wherever congregate the great and the good,' Eric suggested.

Leonard Channing rewarded him with a thin smile that carried no reflection in his eyes. 'Had I known *you* would be here, Eric, I would have thought Martin and Channing well represented, and could have stayed away. But then, we're never quite certain at the board exactly where you are.'

'As a mere part-time director of your board, Leonard, I can hardly desert my practice in Newcastle.'

'Ah yes, your practice. How is the villains and vagabond business in the North?'

'Remarkably similar to merchant banking in the City,' Eric replied.

Their glances locked. The senior partner in Martin and Channing was shorter than Eric: of middle height and now in his early sixties, he had sharp, patrician features and thin, humourless lips. There was no love lost between him and Eric: Channing had the confidence and social ease that enabled him to hide his feelings most of the time, but there were times when anger and resentment sparked in his dark eyes in his dealings with Eric. He had the reputation of being tough, behind an urbane exterior, used to winning arguments; he had never reconciled himself to the manner in which Eric had handled the affair of the *Sea Dawn** and there had been times when he felt he himself had been mistaken in his reaction. In the aftermath of the *Sea Dawn* decisions Channing had suggested Eric take a seat on the board of Martin and Channing, so he could keep an eye on

* *Premium on Death.*

him. There had been times since when Leonard Channing had regretted that decision. Now, with Anne's considerable investment in the bank, it would be difficult to dislodge the man he had once thought he could easily outmanœuvre.

Channing sipped his wine delicately, and glanced away, his lizard eyes surveying the room. 'I'm not sure it's balanced, viewing this glittering assemblage of City talent in comparison with the sleazy clients you deal with in that bizarre practice of yours in Newcastle, but there you are, perhaps I should put your attitude down to crass inexperience.'

'*Gentlemen*,' Anne said firmly,' this is a social occasion, and there is a lady present. No blood-letting, please.'

Channing smiled thinly and saluted her with his glass. 'You're quite right, my dear, I shouldn't allow my sense of social duty to be skewed by my feelings towards a fellow board member—even if he happens to be your husband. How on earth did you come to make such a choice? I realize *we* hadn't met five years ago, but I was and am a widower, you know—'

'Leonard, I had no idea you thought of embracing anything other than takeovers and mergers!'

'Ah, my dear Anne, there are tales I shouldn't tell you, but . . .'

Eric's attention wandered. He looked around the room. The Annual Award for the best Company Report and Accounts, awarded by the International Stock Exchange, attracted a surprisingly influential group of people. The award itself had been an annual event since 1954 as one for the best reports and accounts of public listed companies. It had gained the prestige of age as well as large company support. But the gathering of professionals and businessmen was explained also by the opportunity it allowed many of those on the fringe of business deals to come along and rub shoulders with people who might help in their careers and business. He and Anne were there because Morcomb Estates plc had been nominated in the last six of the award list—and it gave Anne the chance to break away for a few days to London in Eric's company. And it had been pleasant.

Even so, it was not an occasion Eric had been looking forward to: the sweep of the Northumberland hills held a greater attraction after he had been in the City for a few weeks, dealing with a shipping insurance appeal.

The crowd was beginning to thin. Eric realized that people were beginning to move away from the reception area into the Egyptian Room itself, for the award presentation. Leonard Channing was still talking animatedly to Anne and Eric was about to interrupt him, to advise them they should move on, when he realized someone was staring at him. He caught the glance, held it for several seconds.

Like Anne, she was dressed formally, in a dark suit. She was taller than Anne, and her skin was darker, almost swarthy in appearance. She was perhaps thirty-five years of age, with narrow, lean features, a wide, sensuous mouth and dark eyes, bold and challenging. She wore little or no make-up and her chin was lifted, almost arrogantly. She was staring at Eric beneath heavy eyebrows that now seemed to be raised, as though posing a question. She was standing with a small group of men, one of whom was talking animatedly to her but Eric guessed she was barely listening, for her glance sliced past him towards Eric. He felt something move in his stomach, a slow surge of cool, inexplicable excitement at her appraisal. Yet he was also left with the impression that she was measuring him not with the eyes of a woman alone, but of a professional. He smiled slightly at the thought, a little unnerved in addition by the way her glance had affected him and he turned away. 'We'd better move in with the others.'

'Ah, right. You'll forgive me, I know, if I don't join you,' Channing apologized,' but Sir Charles is expecting me to join him in the front row.'

He smiled and slid away, as Anne grimaced at Eric. 'Serves you right. You're not in the front row, are you? You shouldn't needle him so much.'

'Can I help existing?' Eric protested. 'That's all it takes for me to needle Leonard!'

They found seats in the third row and settled themselves as the Deputy Chairman of the International Stock Exchange welcomed the gathering. He introduced the guest speaker before presentation of the awards by the Lord Mayor of London. The guest speaker was a politician: he laced his speech with pedantic jokes about Irishmen and golf. There were polite ripples of laughter even though Eric guessed that everyone had heard the jokes before. Lord Evenhulme was twitching sleepily in his seat just in front of them. Anne nudged Eric with the comment, 'He probably thinks he's back in the House of Lords!'

Eric looked up past the speaker on the dais, past the red and white sashed master of ceremonies behind him, to the glittering mace and sword, the galleried pillars above and the stained glass windows, gleaming redly in the late morning light. It was all a long way distant from the days when he had pounded the beat in Newcastle as a young policeman. Life had changed radically for Eric the day the police surgeon had told him of the onset of glaucoma; but good fortune and hard work had meant he could qualify as a solicitor, stay with the law even if he was seen by many of his erstwhile colleagues as now on the wrong side of the enforcement fence.

And then there had been Anne.

It seemed such a long time ago that he had met her, and resisted the attraction that had welled up between them. Yet their marriage had been satisfying, in spite of the difference in their ages, and their experiences and background. She had learned to temper her idealism to the reality of marriage; he had found that the disappointments of an earlier, failed marriage need not presage an inability to accept happiness from another woman.

It was true that Anne's wealth could still be a barrier between them on occasions, a basis for misunderstanding, as could his insistence upon a Tyneside practice, when it would have been easier to work with and for her. But independence was important to him, even if there were times when it made him feel vaguely guilty. The seat on the board of Martin and Channing was at least a compromise, looking after her interests in the merchant bank.

It had resulted in a curious lifestyle, nevertheless: weekends at a landed estate in Northumberland, a Quayside practice dominated by petty crime and shipping matters, and involvement in the wheeling, dealing world of City investments and international finance transactions.

Curious indeed.

There was a burst of applause.

Startled, Eric realized the speaker was finishing. He glanced involuntarily towards the side of the room, and the girl with dark eyes was staring at him.

She was frowning now, the heavy eyebrows ridged with thought. Eric, his own mind still confused with consideration of his life and marriage, looked away almost guiltily, and then smiled to himself at the realization. The Lord Mayor was on his feet, announcing the award, and Anne was muttering beside him.

'I don't believe it!'

'Hush!'

'But have you seen their presentation of accounts? *Cartoons*, for God's sake!'

There had been, inevitably, speeches of thanks from the recipients of the three prizes awarded. Anne glowered as they droned on: Eric was not aware she had herself prepared a speech against the eventuality of winning, but she clearly felt she could have done better than the portly gentlemen who had won the opportunity. When the eminent barrister who had chaired the panel of judges gave his explanations for the choice she wriggled in dispute; Eric grabbed her hand and squeezed it, trying not to allow his amusement to escape. He was pleased when the final round of applause broke out and they were able to rise.

The celebratory champagne was waiting outside.

'I need this!' Anne scowled.

'I loved your company report, myself,' Eric assured her soberly.

She caught his eye, glared at him for a moment, and then laughed throatily in self-deprecation. 'Oh God, I'm a bad loser, aren't I? Well, to hell with it! Who cares anyway, as long as the champagne is cold?'

'In the Mansion House, it always is!'

The voice was Leonard Channing's. He had returned to join them, but he was not alone this time. He was holding the elbow of a woman taller than himself, who was staring directly at Eric. As she had been staring, intermittently, during the whole of the time in the Egyptian Room.

Leonard Channing smiled coolly. 'Anne, may I introduce to you an acquaintance of mine from the City. Actually, it's Eric she really wants to meet, but protocol demands I first introduce the little woman, don't you agree?'

Anne was now feeling the edge of Leonard's tongue and for a moment Eric thought she was about to rise to the bait. Then the tension in her changed as she smiled sweetly. 'Quite right, Leonard; after all, someone must stay behind to look after the house and garden and it's as well that she is paid attention from time to time.' She switched her attention to Channing's companion. 'But I didn't catch the name.'

'Because Leonard omitted to give it. He was always better at making impressions than introductions . . . My name is Eileen O'Hara. Hardly anyone uses my first name.' She made no secret of the appraisal in her eyes as she looked at

Anne. 'As for house and garden, I'm aware that Morcomb Estates is a pretty big house, and the garden—'

'The estates in Northumberland are *quite* extensive,' Leonard Channing intervened, enjoying himself. 'But it was Eric you asked me to introduce you to.'

Eileen O'Hara glanced at Leonard Channing coolly, then nodded, and extended her hand. 'Mr Ward.'

'I'm pleased to meet you,' Eric replied formally, aware of the stiffness of Anne's back, and unwilling that Leonard should make more out of this situation than was necessary.

'O'Hara . . .' Anne was saying thoughtfully. 'Didn't I read recently . . . you're not the O'Hara who chairs the board of Broadlands?'

The tall young woman with the dark eyes looked at Anne and nodded slowly. 'That's the one.'

'I've heard of you.'

'And I of you,' Eileen O'Hara replied.

'And of my colleague Eric, it would seem,' Leonard chipped in again, mischievously attempting to maintain the tension.

'That's right.' Eileen O'Hara half turned away from Anne, not dismissively, but intimating that she was quite prepared to take up the challenge Leonard was throwing down between the two women. 'I saw you with Mr Channing earlier, and one of my companions from Broadlands guessed you were Eric Ward.'

'So?'

'I was interested in meeting you. I heard a little about the *Sea Dawn* affair.' She glanced at Leonard, and the senior partner in Martin and Channing was made aware by the glance that gossip in the City could run deep and cut sharply. 'And then more recently there was the business of the Salamander Corporation.* It caused quite a stir, Mr Ward. Some powerful fingers got burned.'

---

* *The Salamander Chill.*

'I didn't apply the matches.'

'Maybe not . . . but I hear you lit them,' she said thoughtfully, her eyes holding Eric's. 'And you're still active in the City?'

'On behalf of my wife,' Eric replied, and put one hand on Anne's shoulder. She seemed to resent the gesture, as though she thought it patronizing, and moved slightly away. Eric frowned. 'It's Anne who owns the shares in Martin and Channing: I merely represent her interests on the board.'

'From time to time Mr Ward also represents gangsters on Tyneside.' Channing intervened.

'Hardly that,' Eric suggested, refusing to respond to Channing's needling tone.

'A rich life, nevertheless,' Eileen O'Hara said, smiling.

'And a full one, Miss O'Hara.'

'O'Hara will do. We must talk again some time. This is hardly the occasion, but I'd like to take your . . . advice. Perhaps you'd be prepared to give me a ring at Broadlands. Delighted to meet you, Mr Ward. And Mrs Ward . . .'

Leonard Channing's narrow lips lifted in a wolfish smile as he walked away with the woman who ran Broadlands, to take her back to her companions.

'He enjoyed that,' Anne muttered.

'He was just needling. It's unimportant.'

'You responded to her . . . but with care. I didn't like that. I think my presence inhibited you.'

'Nonsense.'

'*Give me a ring at Broadlands*, indeed!' Anne snorted. 'You'd have chatted her up if I hadn't been here.'

'I don't—'

'*She* wants your advice, but you don't spend too much time advising *me*! Even if I do ask for it. Take the Paulson business, for instance. I've wanted you to act for me over that negotiation but you refuse.'

'It makes more sense for you to take independent legal advice—'

'The kind I imagine you could be giving to Eileen O'Hara?'

Eric paused, looked levelly at his wife and managed a rueful smile. 'Anne, Leonard just set this up to have a crack at me, and he's using you to do it. It's quite pointless—'

'You're right. Why quarrel because another woman gives my husband a few bold glances? I've got other things to do than argue about such trivialities.'

'Anne—'

'I've got to go, anyway. I want to do some shopping. I'll make my own way back to the hotel. See you later.'

'Hold on,' Eric protested. 'You know I can't go yet: I've got to have a word with Edgerton, and—'

'You don't like shopping,' Anne responded sweetly. 'I'll get off to boring old Harrods. I'm leaving the field clear for you. Enjoy the hunting. But watch out for the female sharks. They have the sharpest teeth!'

3

The conversation swirled around the room, the noise levels rising in alcohol-affected cadences as full advantage was taken of the trays of champagne and whisky. Eric stayed with his orange juice, managed to avoid the more obvious bores among his City acquaintances and had a brief conversation with the merchant banker called Edgerton concerning issues which had arisen at the board regarding a tombstoning advertisement placed in the *Financial Times*.

When Edgerton was drawn aside by another banker Eric glanced at his watch. This gathering would stay on for another hour or so yet, at least as long as the drinks held out; on the other hand, Anne would hardly be returning to their hotel for several hours; in the mood she was in on leaving the Mansion House she was likely to spend all afternoon and even longer on her own, and he doubted if he'd see her this side of dinner. It meant he would be at something of a loose end: he was reluctant to show his face at the offices of Martin and Channing after Leonard Channing's gibes concerning his unavailability, but there was no other business he had to transact in London. There was an exhibition at the Tate that looked interesting, but not *that* interesting.

'You look as if you're about to take flight.'

Eileen O'Hara had returned, a mocking smile on her wide mouth, one eyebrow lifted challengingly. She was holding a glass of champagne in her hand, elegantly, and she waved it as she surveyed the rest of the room. 'I can't say I blame you, wanting to escape this lot of stuffed shirts.'

'It's getting late,' Eric offered.

'And the little woman's gone. Shopping?'

'You're absolutely right,' Eric replied, ignoring the gibe.

'So that means you're free to talk with me.'

'If we've something to talk about. I'm not really the small talk kind; boringly, I tend to be interested in business.'

'And that's what I want to talk to you about.' Her bold eyes appraised him, almost belying the words. 'I was serious —what I said earlier. It wasn't just a female line to get your wife edgy—you know, the way one woman likes to step on to another's preserves just for the hell of it. I *do* want to talk to you; I want your advice.'

'I'm a lawyer from Newcastle,' Eric said. 'There are many more here in London, of the hotshot kind, who could be of more assistance, I'm sure. The big city firms—'

'They weren't involved in the Salamander affair. You were.' She sipped the champagne, watching him carefully over the rim of her glass. 'But right now I seem to detect a certain nervous tension. What's the matter? You afraid of me? Or maybe you've been warned off by your wife?'

Eric was unreasonably annoyed. He was aware she was

needling him, mocking him to get a reaction, and he knew also his reaction was precisely what she expected. He was unable to check it, nevertheless. 'My wife doesn't order my business life, and I've no idea what you're talking about when you suggest I might be afraid of you. I've met big girls before.'

She grinned, cast a quick look down her body. Her jacket was open, her full breasts swelling under the white shirtfront. 'Touché. I asked for that. OK, so we've now cleared the air, and it's agreed you're allowed to talk to big girls . . . even to me.'

'Not *allowed*—I *choose* to talk to you,' Eric said and then almost snapped at the words, aware of the trap. 'That's not what I—'

'The hell with it. Let's stop playing with words,' the dark-eyed woman said. 'Look, this isn't a flirtation. I was quite serious when I said earlier that I'd like to have a chat with you about the way things are going at Broadlands. Let's do that.'

'Whenever you wish,' Eric replied but with a degree of reluctance that seemed to challenge her.

'Now?' Her dark eyes were serious, the mockery gone to be replaced by a hard decisive glint. When he hesitated, seeking an excuse, she went on, 'There's nothing here to keep you. Your wife's gone shopping. What's wrong with an hour this afternoon?'

'I suppose there's no reason—'

'OK, but not here. We need somewhere more private. Come with me.'

She turned and walked away from him, confidently, leaving him no alternative but to follow her as she slipped between the groups of red-faced men talking with animation and drinking with enthusiasm. They made way for her, with an occasional murmur and an appreciative glance. She headed towards the far corner of the room, where three men were standing together. As she approached one of them glanced at her, then detached himself from the others. He stepped forward to meet her. She turned, to introduce him to Eric.

'Tom—this is Eric Ward . . . Tom Black. Tom is the vice chairman of Broadlands, a wheeling-dealing tower of strength and my right-hand man.'

They shook hands. Tom Black was of Eric's height, about forty-five years of age, with a golfer's wrist, a surprisingly wind-burned face, wide-set eyes that gave him an air of perpetual surprise and a mouth that smiled easily and charmingly. Eric was too wary to go by initial impressions, but he felt that the man would be a useful one to have in his corner, and a tough one to cross. His grip was firm, though brief: his pale blue eyes appraised Eric swiftly, took an initial view and filed it in a neat, businesslike mind. He half turned to say something to Eileen O'Hara and then stopped, looked back keenly to Eric. He frowned. 'Ward? Of Martin and Channing?'

'I do have other interests,' Eric replied.

'Yes, but you're the Eric Ward who dealt with the Salamander affair.'

'News travels fast.'

'The City is a surprisingly small place.'

'Especially when you want a private conversation,' O'Hara chipped in. 'Tom, I want to whisk Eric away for a conversation. I'll take the car. Can you make your own way back to Broadlands?'

Tom Black stared at her, hesitating. For a moment Eric received the impression that the man was about to protest, or question the nature of the conversation she wanted with Eric, as though he felt he had a right to govern her social decisions. Then, clearly, he changed his mind. Black nodded, his glance slipping away from her back to Eric. 'Surely. No problem. You're leaving at once?'

'As soon as I get my coat. Eric?'

She swept off. Eric hesitated, half smiled at Tom Black

who grimaced. 'She can be quite impulsive. Hope to meet you again, Ward.'

'As you said, the City's a small place.'

He made his way through the thinning crowd and down the stairs to the lobby. Eileen O'Hara joined him a few minutes later. She must have already had a word with the doorman, because as they stepped out into the courtyard the black Jaguar was waiting for them, the uniformed chauffeur impassive in the front seat. She spoke briefly to him as Eric held open the door for her; when he settled down beside her in the back seat Eric glanced sideways at her profile.

'Where are we going?'

'The company flat. We can talk there.'

Female sharks, Anne had warned, had sharp teeth.

It commanded a splendid view of the Docklands area, Tower Bridge and the Thames. The broad sweep of the window displayed the London skyline to advantage: at night the view would be breathtaking. The sitting-room was perhaps thirty feet long, deep carpeted, elegantly furnished and decorated with a professional hand and eye. It was clearly not a flat that would be lived in regularly: it had no worn, lived-in look or signs of personal possessions. But it was comfortable, expensive, and suitable for private meetings between business confederates. Or lovers.

'God, I'm glad to get rid of these!' O'Hara groaned and kicked off her shoes, sending them flying carelessly across the room until they fetched up under the window. She padded across the room towards the sideboard in the corner: there was something about her barefooted movements that was sensuous and catlike. 'Drink?'

'Something soft.'

She frowned, glancing back quizzically over her shoulder. 'Oh yes, I think I heard something . . . you got some kind of problem, is that it?'

'Glaucoma. No great problem these days . . . I'm not

teetotal, but alcohol doesn't help. And now, well, I've got used to taking very little.'

'Not like me. I drink like a fish.'

He didn't believe her. Eric sat down on the brocaded settee as she poured herself a gin and tonic; she brought him a lime and soda and sat down in the easy chair facing him. She raised her glass. 'Here's to a successful business relationship.'

'That's a little premature,' Eric suggested.

'Maybe. But I have a feeling.' Her dark eyes dwelled on his, frankly. 'I've heard about you ... and I like what I see.'

'Appearances can be deceptive,' Eric said shortly. 'And you haven't told me what your problem is. I imagine it's something to do with your company, Broadlands?'

'You can say that again. You know anything about the business?'

'Little, if anything.'

Eileen O'Hara shrugged, sipped her gin, and nodded. 'Right, so maybe I'd better start at the beginning. We're a pretty boring company.'

'Which means?'

'Our main business has always been roof sheeting, clay bricks, concrete tiles and engineering services.'

'Good old-fashioned stuff.'

'But unexciting to the stock market.'

'It turns a good profit, I imagine,' Eric suggested.

'It has done, but for some years that margin has been declining. We've seen an increase in operating profit during the last three years, but that was after a significant slump, after I took over. There'll be some on the board who'll tell you the company's financial rating has got worse rather than better since I took the chair five years ago. They won't say it when I'm in the room.'

Eric smiled. 'Has it—got worse, I mean?'

'It has.' She grinned suddenly and it lit up her face,

making her dark eyes sparkle. 'I have to admit it. And I made my own contribution to that, I agree. We had a few board wrangles, when my father died and I picked up his shareholding and the chair. Some people resent a woman—a youngish woman—stepping into preserves they regard as male.'

'My wife's had similar problems.'

'Mmm . . .' Eileen O'Hara stared at him calculatingly. 'You don't do too much with your wife's company.'

'We keep our business interests separate from our personal lives.'

'That'll be your doing, not hers.'

Eric made no reply.

O'Hara smiled and nodded. 'OK, nothing to do with me. Right, let's give you the Broadlands story. Fact is, the company was built up by my grandfather, then my father held it steady—though little more—and after he died, a widower with me as the only child, he left his shareholding to me and I came in as head of the board. There was some grumbling, we restructured, lost a few people and a lot of money, as our capital expenditure remained high and there was a heavy outflow of funds, and then I took an unpopular decision and bought in—against some opposition—a new managing director. His name is Ted deSoutier. You come across him?'

Eric shook his head.

'No? OK, well, he's a bit of a pusher, you know? Early thirties, good solid background in the fuel distribution industry, short period in the computer business—we got him through a headhunter, and he certainly blew some fresh air into the company. There's no doubt he worked hard, and we did see some returns for all the stripping he did, the leaning on people, the pushing of a new research and development programme.'

'So Broadlands has turned the corner?'

'It's turned *a* corner! The trouble is, the vista then disclosed hasn't exactly seemed like a financial paradise.' O'Hara grimaced prettily; Eric was vaguely surprised at the thought, for he would not have described her as pretty, for all her sensuality. 'In reality,' she continued,' while the results have been basically acceptable, the company has remained . . . well, unexciting.'

'To you?'

She shook her head vigorously. 'No, not at all. I get a hell of a kick out of running my company. No, it's just that our return on capital doesn't exactly inflame our accountants to enthusiasm.'

'Are accountants ever inflamed?'

She laughed. 'That's as may be. Anyway, the fact is that deSoutier has been running things for three years now. During that period he's managed to raise average earnings by sixty per cent, but the share prices still languish. And three weeks ago he came to the board to explain why. It was quite a meeting.'

'The board didn't like his explanation?' Eric asked.

'Not just that.' She frowned, and sipped at her gin and tonic. 'The reasons were those we could have guessed. An unexciting product range; an old-fashioned image, a range of services that no one was going to get excited about.'

'Fortunes have been built on less.'

'We're not making fortunes.' She set down her glass, stood up and folded her arms. She stood with her back to him, gazing thoughtfully out of the window. He could see the curve of her back under her jacket, the line of her thigh outlined in the dark, formal skirt she wore. She had well-turned calves, not elegant, but muscular, and he imagined she would have retained a youthful athleticism as she moved into the sedentary world of company finance.

'No,' she said slowly, 'it wasn't that the board disagreed with his explanation. It was just that his proposal for turning the company around came as a bit of a surprise. Maybe we should have guessed what he'd be saying, in the climate of the City these days. After all, they're common enough.'

'What are?'

'Leveraged buy-outs.'

She was right. They were spreading like a rash in Britain as well as in the United States. A record £3.6 billion had been committed to management buy-outs in the previous twelve months and he had read somewhere that the value of such activity had increased nearly fourteen times since 1984. And the money market was all for it. It seemed to think the words of Sir Thomas Gresham, founding father of the City of London, still had weight: 'It will profitt the citie.'

Eric was silent. O'Hara turned abruptly to face him. She walked the few steps between them until she was standing directly in front of him, blocking his view to the window, staring down at him, her hands now on her hips, drawing back her jacket.

Eric looked up. 'Your managing director proposed to take the company into other private hands?'

'That's it. He put a general proposal to the board which sort of took the wind out of their sails. He suggested that he be allowed to pay off the existing shareholders in a leveraged buy-out. He and two other managers—called Neilson and Daly—proposed to do a deal with an investment bank and buy out the existing shareholders in Broadlands with borrowed money. The idea then would be that we—the shareholders—could take our money and run, while deSoutier would sell off parts of the firm to lower the debt commitments to the investment bank and go on to concentrate upon its core assets. He's convinced—and he sounded convincing—that everyone could benefit. In the short term, we'd get a good price for our shares. As for deSoutier, with a management buy-out like that he felt he would eventually be able to settle the debt and sell the remainder of the company—leaner and fitter—back to the shareholders at a vast profit to the new owners.'

'It's been done before.'

'And often,' Eileen O'Hara agreed. 'It could happen with Broadlands. Anyway, to put it in a nutshell, deSoutier convinced the board. They decided they'd like to see the colour of his bid.'

Eric finished his drink, aware that she was still standing above him, uncomfortably close, staring at him fixedly. 'What was your position in all this?'

She was slow in replying, almost as though she were suddenly thinking of other things. Then she said quietly, 'Interested.'

She could, he felt, be talking about the Broadlands management buy-out or something else.

'How much of his homework has deSoutier really done?' Eric asked.

'You mean has he found investment backing?'

'That's right.'

She made no move to step back, away from him. 'Ted deSoutier made no clear statement about it to the board, but he hinted he already had investment backing. I've made some inquiries since. It looks as though the front runner is the Melling Investment Bank.'

'Pete Corsa.'

'You've heard of him?'

'I've heard his name is really a corruption of Corsair,' Eric said drily.

Eileen O'Hara snorted. 'I've never met him, but I hear similar things. Still, there are many in the City who regularly go to bed with the devil to raise the share prices. Why not Broadlands?'

'Is that the view of the board?'

'They have no view yet. There's no formal proposal before them. Ted deSoutier's still working on it. But he expects to put the papers together fairly soon.'

A short silence fell between them. Eric hesitated. 'It all sounds . . . interesting. I'm not quite certain where I fit into all this.'

'Quite simply. I want your advice.'

'About what?'

Her voice seemed to drop an octave, as a brooding note came into it. 'I have a feeling . . . call it woman's instinct. There's something wrong about the situation. I don't know what it is, and up to now I've trusted Ted deSoutier, but suddenly I have the feeling he's changed, there's something . . . aberrant in his proposal. Is that the right word? I don't know. Or maybe it's because Corsa is involved.'

'I still don't see—'

'There's another problem. We've had to take on a new company secretary. He's inexperienced, as far as Broadlands is concerned. He doesn't inspire me with the greatest confidence, though maybe it's not all his fault. Things were left in a bit of a mess—'

'Your previous company secretary hadn't left a tidy desk?'

Eileen O'Hara was silent for a few moments. 'It was all a bit . . . sudden. One of those things. We had a good man . . . been with the company a long time, knew my father well. Fred Wishart. I trusted him. But . . . well, he was mugged on his way home from the office one night. One of these stupid, blind, unnecessary situations.' She waved her left hand in a sudden, stabbing gesture of frustration. 'It would have been some coked-up youngster, wanting something for another fix. The police think Wishart tried to put up a struggle. He was knifed.'

'Killed?'

She nodded. 'It left things a bit awry. We had to get a replacement. I'm short on advice, right now.'

'I'm not sure it's the kind of advice I can give.'

'I want you in my corner,' she insisted.

'This isn't really my field.'

'You've got instincts. I've heard about them. The *Sea Dawn* and Salamander situations have given you a certain reputation in the City whether you believe it or not. There's a view you were lucky as much as smart. So maybe I'm gambling as far as your skills are concerned, but I certainly like to have lucky men around me. So, I want to retain you, as a legal adviser, while this management buy-out is proceeding. I have a . . . feeling you can help.'

'It sounds tenuous, as a reason.'

'Not to me.' She stared down at him. There was a certain huskiness in her voice as she spoke. 'Will you come on board?'

Eric hesitated. 'I'll think about it.' Slowly, almost reluctantly, he rose to his feet. Eileen O'Hara made no move to step back. Even in her stockinged feet she was only a little shorter than him and her face was only inches from his. He could see a languor in her dark eyes, and he was aware of the closeness of her body. There was a delicate hint of perfume in his nostrils; her mouth was very close, and now very soft. 'But no promises.'

'I'll send you some papers,' she said, almost whispering. 'Then you can decide. Meanwhile . . .'

Before he could move, her arms slid gently around his neck and she raised her face to his. She kissed him, and as her mouth closed over his he responded to the softness of her touch and the flickering of her tongue, aware of the pressure of her breasts and the warmth of her body, curving sinuously against him. His blood stirred and his body moved. They stood together like that for several seconds, then slowly she disengaged herself.

He looked at her steadily, concealing the pounding in his veins. 'Satisfying your curiosity?'

She wasn't fooled by his coolness. 'Maybe I was sealing a bargain.'

He shook his head. 'Not yet. I've plenty on my plate, here in London and also in the North . . . but I'll think about your proposal.' He turned away. 'Thanks for the drink . . . and the conversation. I'd better be getting back.'

Eileen O'Hara was still standing there, staring steadily at him as he reached the door. He paused, looked back to her as a thought struck him. 'This character deSoutier . . . you say you no longer trust him.'

'That's right.'

'He was your appointment.'

'He was.'

'No woman's instinct on that occasion?'

She smiled, almost feline in her recollection. 'It was, as I recall . . . very instinctive. He caused . . . vibrations, at that time. He's changed. Or maybe I have.' Her smile widened. 'Grown up, perhaps.'

Eric thought of the way her body had curved against his and he smiled back at her, wryly. 'I wonder if there was ever a time when you weren't grown up.'

'Even little girls learn how to manipulate men.'

'And their skills increase with age?'

'Not their skills. Their weapons.'

Eric opened the door.

'I'll be in touch,' she said.

He almost hoped she wouldn't.

CHAPTER 2

1

The distant thunder of an RAF jet on a low-flying training flight beyond Otterburn rolled along the valley below them, echoing briefly among the crags of the hillside before fading against the birdsong in the trees. The morning was bright, the sun sparkling on the narrow strip of white that tipped the Cheviot, an overnight fall of snow on the high ground that had already disappeared on the lower slopes to leave them glistening under the horses' hooves as Anne and Eric rode early on the fell.

It was a relaxation they both enjoyed, a complete change from the pressures that crowded in upon them separately. Morcomb Estates, with its landholdings, investments and business interests was taking up more and more of Anne's time and attention: she did not see herself as a passive member of the board that controlled her inheritance. Eric's own practice in Newcastle was busy, with a significant increase in business from the shipping companies that still saw Tyneside as an important centre, and he had taken on an extra assistant to deal with the details of the growing criminal side. The bridge that lay between himself and Anne in business terms was through his situation with Martin and Channing, where Eric's position on the board was as her representative. Even so, there was a tendency for the activity to place a distance between them, necessarily because of his absences from the North-East to attend to board affairs at the investment bank in London.

A weekend morning ride was therefore important to both of them: tensions were eased, they had the opportunity to take exercise together, and there was the enjoyment of the clean sweep of the hills, the sharpness of the morning air, and the opportunity to put aside business matters, and relax.

They rode side by side, companionably, not speaking, until they reached Arnold's Farm and then rode to the high fell in single file, leaving bruise marks on the damp grass until they picked up the narrow stony track that opened out the valley before their eyes. When they reached the cropped moorland at the top of the fell the sky was a sharp blue above them, there was a distant vapour trail pencilled along the horizon and the horses were blowing hard.

'We had a meeting of the Morcomb board on Friday,' Anne said abruptly, shading her eyes with her left hand as she looked about her.

'I didn't know you had one scheduled,' Eric said

cautiously. It was unlike Anne to start discussing business when they were out riding like this: the subject had become almost taboo, since they both needed time to relax and enjoy each other's company without reference to their professional lives.

'It's the Paulson business,' she replied shortly, and fell silent.

The saddle creaked as Eric shifted his weight. His mount snorted, and the animal's breath silvered the air. 'Have you managed to discover the extent of the indebtedness yet?' Eric asked, realizing that Anne, uncharacteristically, wanted to talk about it.

'It's bloody four million, isn't it!' she said gloomily.

'As much as that?'

'We've had the final survey reports—the defects are pretty extensive, and the main problem is that the costs we'll incur in putting them right, bearing in mind inflation over the last four years, will push our liabilities higher than we might have expected.'

Eric made no reply. He had seen how the matter had gnawed at Anne over recent months. It was not that the whole business could be laid at her door, but she had shown a certain liking for the plausible Eddie Paulson. When the contracts for the building of the marina at Amble had first been negotiated Paulson had been a visitor to Sedleigh on several occasions. In his mid-thirties, with a reputation as a high flyer in the construction business, he had proved to be a witty and entertaining guest with an easy smile and a teasing, effervescent manner. Anne had been won over by his charm, though Eric doubted that it would have influenced her business judgment; in any case, the rest of the Morcomb board had looked carefully at the whole project and had certainly not been led by the nose. There were still board members who wriggled uneasily at having a woman as chairman—as there were, it seemed, on the board of Broadlands, where Eileen O'Hara reigned.

Eric dismissed her from his mind, vaguely uneasy at the unbidden entry she had made to his thoughts.

'Paulson is being pretty sticky,' Anne went on. 'He's denying liability, of course, suggesting that the faults lie with his sub-contractors, particularly with the steel deliveries, but the legal advice we have is that primary liability still lies with him.'

'Four million is a lot of money, Anne. What action has the board decided to take?'

She leaned forward to stroke her animal's neck. She shook her head. 'What else could they decide, other than to take proceedings against him?'

'Sue? For four million? It'll bankrupt him.'

'So what other choice do we have? The man's a fraud, I'm convinced of that now! A plausible character, a smooth talker, but he conned us, Eric, with the plans and the projections of costs. And I've more than a suspicion that he'll have salted away significant sums within the contract: the accountants are looking at it, and my guess is they'll come up with something pretty damaging.'

'I wouldn't count on it, love. Paulson's no fool: he'll have covered his tracks pretty well.'

She grunted moodily, and sat there frowning at the hills ahead of them. A patch of dark shadow was tipping the Cheviot, a single cloud high in the sky, and she stared at it, as though it reflected her mood. Some of the exhilaration of the morning left Eric too; her raising the Paulson affair was significant in itself when they were out riding, putting business behind them, but he now began to wonder if she had other things on her mind as well as a four million pound lawsuit.

She pulled her horse around. She did not meet Eric's glance. 'I've had enough,' she said. 'Let's go down.'

Anne was still busying herself at the stables while Eric showered and changed; when she came up to take a shower herself he had gone down to the library and was settled in a leather armchair to read the morning newspaper. She did not join him, but shortly before midday he wandered out on to the terrace to find her sitting on the low wall in the sunshine, staring down to the meadow below with a gin and tonic in her hand. She glanced towards him as he came out. 'Drink?'

'I'll get myself a whisky in a moment.'

'We have the Lord Lieutenant to dinner this evening,' she warned. 'You'll be drinking then?'

'I'll abstain.' Eric grinned. 'It might encourage the Lord Lieutenant to slow down—he might even make his way to his car unassisted, then!'

Anne stared at her glass, unresponsively. 'This Paulson business bothers me, Eric.'

'I know.'

'I think you could help.'

'Any way I can.'

'Will you act for the board?'

She had not looked at him when she asked the question. Eric hesitated: this was an old bone of contention. 'I don't think that's wise,' he suggested.

Her brow was clouded. 'The fact you're my husband doesn't mean that you can't help us. It's not a matter of nepotism.'

'It's a matter of independence—and expertise. Fraud is a complicated specialism: petty crime and shipping is one thing—a four million pound fraud lawsuit is another. I don't think it would be right, Anne.'

She raised her chin, squinted up at him in the sunshine. 'All right, so if you won't act for Morcomb—and me—I'll have to use someone else. Like Davison.'

Eric hesitated, then turned and walked back into the house. He poured himself a glass of whisky from the decanter and topped it up with soda, then returned to the terrace. Anne looked at him challengingly: she was not going to let the matter drop.

'You know my views about Davison,' Eric said quietly.

'I know you don't like him—but you've never explained why,' Anne countered.

'It's nothing to do with liking,' Eric insisted. 'Look, it's not easy to explain ... The legal profession has its mad dogs like any other profession; it has its high flyers, its experienced professionals, and a few brilliant men and women too. But the Davisons of this world don't fit into any of those categories.'

'So how do *you* describe Davison?' Anne demanded.

'It's not easy. On the face of things he's an extremely able lawyer—'

'With a highly successful practice!'

'He's a young man who's moved fast, and some would say too fast,' Eric replied stubbornly. 'He married well—'

'He's not alone in that!'

Eric paused, and looked steadily at his wife. 'He married a woman a great deal older than himself, who was already ill, and who died leaving him a solid base to build up a county practice. His clients are wealthy, his business is aristocratic—but he's never proved himself as a lawyer because he's never had to.'

'This sounds remarkably like sour grapes. Do you resent his situation, just because you had to struggle for your own? Your own practice is hardly in his category, is it?'

Eric stared at her coolly, then shook his head. 'What's this about, Anne? I thought we were talking about Davison, not me.'

She flushed, angry with herself and with him. 'We are, and let's stick to that! You won't act for Morcomb, but you object to my suggestion that we go to one of the leading lawyers on Tyneside—'

'It depends on your definition of "leading"!'

'But you still haven't said what you've got against him!'

'He's . . . shallow. All right, I know that's a vague reply to make but I have to say that for all his success, and his credibility among his business and aristocratic clients, in the profession itself he doesn't rate highly.'

'The jealousy of old and less successful men?'

'I don't believe that's so. It's true that some might envy the speed with which his firm has grown, but there have been more than a few incidents, a few hints around the town, that Charles Davison cuts corners—'

'Is that a bad thing?'

'Cutting legal corners can be dangerous—for the client as well as for the lawyer himself. Look, you're putting me on the spot, Anne, because I can't substitute what I'm trying to say, but there's a feeling in the profession that Davison isn't all that he makes himself out to be. He doesn't carry the trust of his fellow professionals.'

'I can't say that his fellow professionals have ever struck me as being exactly a trusting bunch,' Anne sneered. 'Are you sure that we really aren't talking about jealousy here?'

Slowly, Eric said, 'I don't quite know what we *are* talking about. I get the impression there's a hidden agenda to this conversation. I know you're upset about the Paulson business; I don't quite know why you're being so aggressive about my views regarding Charles Davison.'

Anne stared at him, as though struggling with herself. She set down her glass. 'All right. You haven't said a damned word about Eileen O'Hara.'

'Ah.'

'What's that mean?'

'It just meant . . . ah!'

'God, you're so infuriating, you know that, Eric? There are times when you close yourself off to me, treat me like a child, behave as though I've no right to be part of your life! Don't go all enigmatic with me now—I want to know about the O'Hara woman, and I want to know why you've said nothing about her to me.'

'And is that what's behind the rest of it?'

'Never mind the rest of it! I swore to myself I wouldn't ask, but now I have. So talk to me!'

Eric smiled, and sat down on the wall beside her. He put his hand gently on her shoulder. She stiffened, but she did not twist away from him. 'All right, let's talk . . . but let's be clear, too, that the reason why I've not mentioned her to you is that there was little or nothing to say. At the Mansion House, after you left, Eileen O'Hara came back to see me—'

'I knew she would!'

'—and we talked business. She explained that she has certain problems with her company—Broadlands—and that there's a proposal coming forward for a management buy-out. There are aspects about it which bother her, and there's a further problem in that some of the compliance information she might have needed simply isn't available because the company secretary—a chap called Wishart—was killed a little while back.'

'Killed?'

'Murdered. A mugging. It's left a hiatus at officer level in the company.'

'So how do you fit in?'

'That was my question to her. She said she wanted me to act in an advisory capacity.'

'You've no experience in management buy-outs.'

'She suggested she's influenced by my . . . reputation at Martin and Channing. But I think it's thin, as a reason. I don't believe I have anything to offer Broadlands, and I'm not sure I want to get involved.'

'So you're not going to act for them?'

'It's not on my agenda,' Eric said.

'You sound reluctant.'

'I don't mean to be. I've plenty on my plate.'

'Which means you won't act for Morcomb either, in the Paulson suit?'

'If I don't think I have the expertise to help out at Broadlands, I certainly don't consider I have the fraud expertise to deal with Paulson.'

Anne frowned. 'I don't believe I like Morcomb and Broadlands to be bracketed in your thinking.'

'And I consider that you'd be making a mistake over Charles Davison.'

'I think you're just jealous of his success in practice.'

Eric was unable to hold back the words. 'And I get the marked impression that you're not distinguishing between Broadlands and Eileen O'Hara.'

When he settled down at his desk at the Quayside office on Monday morning Eric was still bothered by the events of the weekend. The conversation on the fell and on the terrace had remained with them, hanging in the background and souring the atmosphere during dinner on the Saturday evening. The Lord Lieutenant had noticed nothing: as long as the Chablis, Vouvray and crusted port held out he remained largely unconscious of the tensions that might surround him. His wife, a sharp-eyed elderly lady with a great affection for Anne, had certainly been aware of the atmosphere, however, and had called an early end to the evening. Anne had remained, thereafter, somewhat withdrawn: politely cool, and somewhat distant. No further reference was made to Charles Davison or Eileen O'Hara.

Concentration upon papers on his desk was not easy, so he was pleased when it was time to go to court. Eric was defending a young layabout called Jerome. The case against him was a double one: he had gone to the Hydraulic Engine and bought some drinks for several cronies. When it came to payment he had tendered a fifty-pound note. The barman had accepted it but was suspicious so had called over an off-duty policeman to take a look at the note. It had resulted in Jerome's arrest—when he was found to be carrying cannabis.

The hearing was quickly over. Eric pleaded that Jerome himself had been cheated over the money, but the defence was always going to be a thin one. Jerome claimed he'd bought two fifty-pound notes for £40—that in itself damned him.

'Two and a half years for tendering and deception and three months concurrent for carrying a Class B drug,' the opposing lawyer remarked to Eric as they left the court. 'Could have been worse, old son, could have been worse.'

Eric walked back down the hill to the Quayside. The traffic was heavy, but once he reached Dog Leap Stairs he was able to stroll on in a more leisurely fashion. He stopped for a few minutes, leaning on the wall and looking down over the river. There were two Dutch freighters moored there, and in the distance he caught the sound of the North Sea Ferry booming its farewell as it headed downstream to the bar at Tynemouth. He regretted his words to Anne—an unnecessary lashing back at her own uncertainties. He regretted also the meeting with Eileen O'Hara at the Broadlands company flat. Nothing important had happened, and yet his thoughts returned to it, too often for comfort. He could remember the touch of her mouth on his, and he resented the memory. Yet he also resented Anne's attitude, over O'Hara, and over Charles Davison and the Paulson fraud.

But there was no relief when he got back to the Quayside. He groaned when he saw who was sitting in the waiting-room. The receptionist pursed her lips and looked at him sadly over her glasses. 'I'm sorry, Mr Ward. He insisted on waiting to see you.'

Eric glared at the slightly built, crumpled, grey-haired man who had risen sheepishly to his feet. 'Trouble again, Garrity?'

''Fraid so, Mr Ward.'

Eric sighed. 'All right, give me ten minutes, and then you'd better come up and tell me all about it.'

Eric made his way to his office, discarded his topcoat and went into the washroom. The pilocarpine was standing there on the shelf: he always kept a supply in the office in case he suffered a sudden attack. The telltale, familiar prickling at the back of his eyes had started in the courtroom this morning, partly the result of tension. It was as well to take remedial action before it became too bad. He held his head back and applied the eye drops.

His secretary knew him well enough to have a cup of coffee waiting for him when he returned to his room. He sat staring moodily out of the window, sipping the coffee, then decided he'd better see Garrity sooner than later. He buzzed reception, and told them to send the Irishman up.

Garrity took the seat facing Eric with the familiarity of someone who had been to the office often enough in the past. His grey cheeks were unshaven with a two days' stubble; his collar was frayed and his shirt cuffs dirty. There was a yellowish tinge to his eyes, but he had an air of relief, as though merely having the opportunity to talk to Eric meant that some of his troubles were over.

'So, don't tell me you're the victim of circumstance, Garrity. I thought you were going straight.'

'But believe me, Mr Ward, that's exactly the size of it,' Garrity protested. He had an Irish brogue, retained in spite of thirty years' residence on Tyneside, and it tended to become more marked when he was excited. 'I told you last time, when you got me off that receiving charge, that it was the strait and narrow for me from now on.'

'So what's gone wrong?'

'To be sure, it's just circumstance, like you say! You'll have heard, no doubt, that I got a good job.'

Eric frowned. 'I seem to remember . . . didn't you pick up a job as an office cleaner?'

'That's right, Mr Ward.' An element of pride had oozed into Garrity's tone. 'You was kind enough to drop them a

A NECESSARY DEALING

line, and I got the job, and I been holding it for seventeen months now. A steady day, a steady wage.'

'So what's gone wrong?' Eric asked. A sudden suspicion took him. 'It's not the damned horses again, is it?'

Garrity scratched his cheek and ducked his head sheepishly. 'Now then, Mr Ward, you got to understand a man like me, with the kind of deprived background I got. I was brought up in Waterford, and me grandfather was a man who actually knew Mick the Miller! Finest dog that ever ran a race! Now me, I was never struck with the dogs, but coming here to Newcastle meant that the racecourse was on me doorstep, and the racing was in my veins and it's more than flesh and blood can stand—'

'You'd better tell me the facts,' Eric interrupted. 'Save the tears for the judge. What's happened? You've been losing at the track, you've gone back to your old ways—'

'No, no, it's not like that, Mr Ward,' Garrity protested. 'I've had a good run at the track, believe me! I got to know one of the stable lads over at Gosforth Park and he's put me in the way of some pretty good tips. Sure, a few of them didn't do as well as expected, but if you take the rough with the smooth, I reckon over the last year or so I must be in by maybe three, four hundred quid.'

'Which you'll have spent.'

'Got to celebrate a win with your friends, Mr Ward.'

'So what's the problem?'

'Well, I think they're being unreasonable, and I don't see how they can prove . . . I mean exactly prove that it was anything to do with me—'

'What is it you think they can't prove, Garrity?' Eric asked wearily. 'Come on, get to the point.'

'The phone calls, sir.'

'What phone calls?'

'From the offices of the clients.'

Eric stared at the Irishman uncomprehendingly for a

moment, then a small suspicion grew in his mind as he thought of the addiction of the man to horse racing. 'You've been working for a cleaning firm. They've been sending you out to office premises.'

'That's right, Mr Ward, and I did a good job.'

'And then your employers began to get complaints.'

'I don't see how they can be sure it's me. Just because I got a record. It's victimization—'

'The clients had begun to complain to your employers about certain discrepancies in their phone bills?'

'Well, yes, but—'

Eric raised a hand, silencing Garrity. He leaned back in his chair, staring at the Irishman. 'All right, let me paint the scene. You tell me if I'm right. Never mind the excuses —let's look at facts. You're employed by a cleaning firm; you spend some hours in certain clients' offices; their phone bills start to rise. Garrity, you've been using those clients' phones to carry out off-course betting. Is that it?'

'I don't see how they can prove that, Mr Ward—'

'Is that what you've been doing?'

'Well . . .'

'*Is it?*'

Garrity wriggled uncomfortably. 'You got to remember, Mr Ward. They was good tips, and I been doing well—'

'But not well enough to pay back the money you owe for the telephone calls made on other people's phones?'

'I got my expenses,' Garrity protested in an injured tone. 'And a few phone calls . . . it can't be right, the amount they're talking about—'

'How much, Garrity?'

'I mean, British Telecom, the rates they charge—'

'*How much?*'

'Fifteen hundred nicker, Mr Ward.'

'Hell's flames!' Eric exploded. 'You spent fifteen hundred pounds on phone calls alone, to show a working profit of three hundred? How long has this been going on?'

'Just over a year, Mr Ward, but I swear—'

Eric shook his head. 'Never mind the swearing. Have the police been called in?'

Garrity shrugged. 'Don't think so, sir. No need for that. But there's no way I can find fifteen hundred—'

'I doubt if the clients will chase you, Garrity, though the cleaning firm might. The clients will go for your employers' throat!'

'That's the size of it, Mr Ward. Me employers, they're being sued, and I hear they're going to ask you to represent them. I just wanted to get in first, give you my side of the story. I wouldn't want you thinking bad of me, not after the way you've helped me, Mr Ward. You'll do what you can for them, sir?'

'If they instruct me,' Eric said grimly.

'And you . . . er . . . you won't blow no whistles on me, Mr Ward?'

'I would be representing your employers, Garrity, not you. But . . .' Eric paused, glowering at the Irishman. 'If I can help it, there'll be no whistle-blowing.'

'You're a gentleman, Mr Ward.' Garrity beamed. 'A real gentleman . . . I've always said so.'

Eric doubted whether the people to whom Garrity would have said it would move in the kind of influential circles where such a reference might be useful. He suggested Garrity get the hell out of his office, and await events.

The interview with Garrity unsettled Eric further. He was annoyed with himself for thinking it, but he could not avoid the thought that Charles Davison's practice would see few if any Paddy Garritys. In the few short years that Davison had built up his practice, after his wealthy wife died, he had kept an office in the best part of town—unlike Eric on the Quayside—and had deliberately cultivated the social set. Eric despised him for it, but was forced to admit that the practice had flourished. His own was sound enough, but many of his clients were from the West End of Newcastle, and a criminal practice was never the way to a fortune anyway. Shipping contracts and marine insurance were lucrative enough, of course, but did not exactly bring him entry to the drawing-rooms that invited Charles Davison. Eric's presence in them was due to Anne's position: Eric did not resent that, but the thought that his wife was going to use Davison was a sour one.

He tried to concentrate on the papers on his desk, but found it difficult. He called his secretary in and dictated a few letters, took another cup of coffee, and brooded. The fact that Anne seemed to be trying to balance Davison against Eileen O'Hara was annoying: the two were separate issues, and to link them in the way she had could lead to an extension of the argument, and the problem.

'Evening paper's in, Mr Ward.'

The shorthand-typist walked into the room and dropped the newspaper on his desk. She asked him if there was any general typing; then she asked if she could leave the office early. Eric nodded distractedly. He picked up the paper and began to leaf through it in a desultory manner. He would not be returning to Sedleigh tonight: he'd stay at the flat and take some files back with him to work on. Anne was still at the Hall: he'd given her a ring later.

On the business page there was a photograph of Eileen O'Hara.

He stared at it. She was walking out of a building in the City; her head was half turned as though she was saying something to a reporter to her left. She was smiling, and the clean line of her profile reminded him of the afternoon in the Broadlands flat. He recalled again the warmth of her mouth, and its softness.

Irritatedly, he glanced at the headline, and the copy below.

MANAGEMENT BUY-OUT AT BROADLANDS

Eileen O'Hara, chairman of the board at Broadlands, today announced that the company she inherited from her father is to be the subject of a management buy-out bid. It has been rumoured for some time that all was not well at Broadlands as its earnings ratio came under heavy pressure. The bid is a surprise in the City, nevertheless, and it is clear that the managing director, Ted deSoutier, who was not available for comment today, will be central to the bid. No information has been given about the likely investment house backing the bid, nor the extent of the leverage in the buy-out. But it must be more than likely that when one finance house is interested, there'll be others waiting in the wings. Are we going to see a contest in this one? Much depends on whether deSoutier's share bid is seen by the City as a true reflection of the value and potential of Broadlands. Eileen O'Hara is keeping tight-lipped about that at this stage but it can be only a matter of days before the rumours start to fly. And that means we could see some movement in the share prices for Broadlands pretty soon—even against a background which has seen them lift off their base in a gradual rise over the last few weeks.

There was no mention of Pete Corsa and his investment bank.

Eric stared again at the photograph of Eileen O'Hara. The announcement had now been made, and she would soon be making her decisions about the buy-out. That could leave him with a decision too, if his phone rang.

2

Entry to the tower block required a telephone check and the issue of a ticket which showed Eric's destination: the executive suite. The lobby was intimidating: his footsteps echoed on the marble floors and the guards who paced the perimeter turned their heads to stare at him. A drinking fountain on the wall produced a creamy jet from a carved Buddha figure and there was something ceremonious about the chandeliers and seats of marble and echoes. All it lacked was a ceremony.

Armed with his pass, Eric approached the cordoned-off entry point to the lifts. In spite of the guards behind him, the only person now barring his way was a slightly built, dark-haired young woman in a neat blue uniform. An illegal visitor would have found it easy to push past her. Perhaps she had orders to scream.

She checked his pass and entered the lift with him. He smiled at her but obtained no response. When the lift came almost silently to a stop she pressed the button to open the doors and stepped out ahead of him.

'Last door on the left, Mr Ward,' she said quietly, and re-entered the lift.

The carpet on the corridor floor was expensive, as befitted the executive area of Broadlands. Before he was half way along the corridor a door opened and a young woman stepped out to welcome him. She had grey eyes, a practised smile, and a cool profile. 'If you step in here Mr Ward, Miss O'Hara will join you in a few minutes.'

A mahogany, clean-swept desk stood in front of the light-curtained windows which gave an eastern view over the City. The coffee table bore an elegantly patterned set of china beside which was a silver coffee-pot. The grey-eyed girl didn't even bother to ask: she poured a cup for him, smiled again and left the room. He'd almost expected her to say 'Have a nice day.'

The furniture was expensive, the décor tasteful, but the pictures on the wall were surprisingly clinical in their modernity. He failed to understand what message they were supposed to convey, but then, he was a lawyer, not an art critic. The latest company report lay on a small side table; beside it was a copy of *Vogue*. Eric added some cream to his coffee and picked up the company report. He heard the door open behind him.

'Eric. I'm glad you could make it.'

Eileen O'Hara walked towards him with her hand outstretched. He noted her swarthiness again and the bold confidence of her glance: she was not beautiful, but she was elegant. She was wearing a dark wool dress that showed off her figure to perfection. A silver brooch gleamed on her left breast; apart from that she wore no jewellery, and she had clearly used no make-up. Her hair was bright, and her welcoming smile confident. She was in her business world, and in charge of the situation.

Eric put down the report and shook hands with her. She turned aside and poured herself a cup of coffee, gestured towards the armchair near the window and took the chair facing him. 'Thanks for coming in a little early. I thought it would be useful to have a brief chat before the others arrived for the board meeting. A good trip down?'

He had flown. He didn't care for flying but on this occasion he had considered that the fifty-minute trip from Newcastle Airport was better than the three-hour train journey. It gave him less time to dwell on the gnawing doubts he had experienced ever since Eileen O'Hara had phoned him at Sedleigh Hall.

A week ago he had told Anne he had no intention of acting as a Broadlands adviser. Anne had not seen that as an olive branch, or in any sense a bargaining point; a few days later she had told him, somewhat aggressively, that her board had decided to instruct Charles Davison in the Paulson fraud suit. He knew that in reality it was her decision. Maybe Eric should not have responded the way he did, but the anger he felt at her refusal to take his advice about Davison had spilled over when O'Hara rang him.

His anger had been unreasonable, he knew. If he was refusing to act as a legal adviser to Morcomb Estates himself, why should he resent the board following Anne's lead and instructing Davison? He was being selective in his advice. On the other hand, there had been a certain aggressiveness in the manner in which Anne had told him of the Morcomb decision; it had been almost a challenge. Nevertheless, when Eileen O'Hara rang him, he had still been inclined to turn her down. Perhaps she had sensed his inclination; maybe it was why, before he could declare his intention, she had said sweetly, 'I suppose you've had a word with your wife about working for me.'

'What's it got to do with her?' he had asked defensively, even though he knew he was being manipulated. 'I don't work for Morcomb Estates.'

'I just wondered whether she might have considered there could be some conflict of . . . interest,' O'Hara had purred over the phone.

'None,' he had snapped, aware even then that he was being ensnared. She had known what she was doing. So had he.

'Well, I really *do* need some independent advice of the kind you can supply,' she had said, 'because although the deSoutier bid is in, and will be discussed by the board next week, we now understand there's a rival bid. So . . . are you available?'

'I'm available,' Eric had replied doggedly.

Anne had not been pleased.

Eileen O'Hara, on the other hand, was decidedly pleased. She sat in front of him now in her own office, sipped her coffee, and smiled. 'I've got some papers for you, to bring you up to date with the situation, but you can read them later at your leisure. They're in this file. For now, before the board meeting, I think it would be a good idea if I sketched out the situation for you.' She paused reflectively. 'Ted deSoutier has now put in his bid: the offer he's making has the backing of Pete Corsa's investment bank, as you know. The bid amounts to an offer of approximately thirty million. You'll find the details in the file. I'd appreciate your views on them, particularly the points I've marked.'

Eric frowned. 'What's the share price he's offering?'

'Seventy pence per share.'

'I haven't checked this morning's prices, but does deSoutier's offer give you a premium over the market price?'

'Quite a good one, the board thought at its informal meeting last week. The premium's about thirty per cent above market price.'

Eric nodded thoughtfully. 'The City analysts have been suggesting, on the other hand, that your share prices probably don't reflect true values.'

'That's right. There's been a steady rise for some time, so someone's been investing in us and sees us as a good risk, but we're still undervalued.'

'So which way will the board jump this morning in response to deSoutier's bid?' Eric asked.

'Remains to be seen. I think, in general, they're in favour of acceptance of the offer. However . . . I understand there's a new element in the equation.'

'Another bid?'

'One of our directors—Hall Davies—who used to be in charge of sales at one time, a bright, entrepreneurial kind of guy, he rang me two days ago. He told me he hopes to be putting some initial figures before the board today, by way of a competitive bid.'

'Do you know who's making the bid?'

She paused for a moment, eyeing him thoughtfully. 'It's Simon Wells.'

'The arbitrageur?'

'I believe some people use rather different words to describe him.'

'Pete Corsa and Simon Wells,' Eric mused. 'That could lead to an interesting battle. As I understand it, there's little love lost between those two.'

Eileen O'Hara nodded. 'They've snarled at each other

often enough in the past to lead me to believe there might be a little bit of a grudge match coming up here.'

'Which could be to the benefit of the shareholders in Broadlands.'

'Possibly.' She hesitated, then looked at him coolly. 'On the other hand, some of us might be more interested in the future welfare of the company itself, rather than the loot we might get by selling our shares to the highest bidder.'

Eric looked at the woman who held the controlling interest in Broadlands. He was seeing her in rather a different light from the last occasion they had met: then, he had been very aware of her as a woman first and foremost, albeit a somewhat predatory one. Now, there was a different image being presented to him: her tones were serious and clinical, and there was no hint of coquetry in her voice. This was business, *her* business, and nothing else. He liked what he heard.

They spent the next ten minutes discussing the history of Broadlands and the manner in which Ted deSoutier had begun to drag the company out of the doldrums during the last two years. Performance had still not come up to the expectations of some of the board, and the deSoutier offer was certainly being taken seriously. It was, nevertheless, rather interesting that a leveraged buy-out expert like Simon Wells was interested in taking a hand in the game.

Eileen O'Hara glanced at her watch. 'I think it's time we went in: the others will be here by now.'

The boardroom lay across the corridor. It was surprisingly stark in its appearance: located in a corner of the tower block owned by Broadlands, it was sparsely furnished with a long table and chairs with the standard pads, glasses and decanters, but there had been no attempt at lightening the businesslike atmosphere. Eileen O'Hara tapped a chairback near the door, suggesting Eric sat down, and then proceeded to take the chair with its back to the window. A slim, fair-haired young man in a dark pinstripe took the seat to her left. He had the minute book open in front of him. He would be the new company secretary, Eric guessed.

There were three other men in the room; they took their seats as Eileen O'Hara spoke. 'I think we can open the meeting now. I believe I advised each of you separately that I have asked Mr Eric Ward to attend the meeting as an observer on my behalf. He's a lawyer who may be known to some of you: his function here is to act as my adviser and he will play no part in the general discussion. However, I should first introduce him to each of you. On my right, Mr Ward, is Tom Black, deputy chairman of Broadlands. You have already met, of course, at the Awards ceremony at the Mansion House.'

Black turned his tanned face towards Eric and smiled a welcome: his pale blue eyes were friendly, and he nodded. 'Welcome to Broadlands, Ward.'

'The gentleman beside Tom is Hall Davies.'

The ex-sales director was a tall man in his early forties, well over six feet in height, broad-shouldered, built like an American football player with a broken nose to match. His hair was thick and sandy and his eyes heavy-lidded, almost sensuous in appearance. Women would find him attractive for a certain lazy insouciance he adopted in his manner, but his glance was sharp. He seemed to be watching Eric almost challengingly; their glances held for a few seconds, as though he was summing him up in a calculating way. Then he leaned forward and showed his teeth beneath the thick moustache he affected. His voice was deep and resonant, calculated to please. 'Nice to meet you, Ward. I hope you'll follow what's going on. I'm not too clear, myself.'

The man facing him, seated at the other side of the table, snickered. 'I thought you'd be doing most of the talking today, Hall, in view of the fact that you're the one with the counter-proposals to match against deSoutier. If *you* don't know what they mean, how the hell are we supposed to fathom them out?' He turned his glance to Eric. 'My name's Andrew Strain. By training, an accountant, but that was a long time ago. By inclination, a hedonist, but I've never seemed to have the time or energy to misbehave myself with the fleshpots. Perforce, I'm a businessman, but a cautious one. That's where the track of the accountant leads you, I guess.'

He was small, compact and neat of habit and dress; about fifty years old, he was careful about his appearance; his build was slim, probably owing something to the gymnasium; his hair was carefully parted and his smile carefully arranged. His accountancy training would allow him to do nothing without calculation, and hedonism would be the furthest from his inclinations. That he made a joke of his lifestyle interested Eric: already, the man was dissembling, perhaps resentful that Eric had been allowed entry to the boardroom while important issues were being discussed. Eric guessed he would find no friendship from that quarter.

'Well, shall we begin?'

Eileen O'Hara took them through the preliminaries, breaking off at an appropriate moment to introduce the company secretary, John Leslie, to Eric. It was an afterthought that seemed to emphasize the man's relatively brief period with the company, having taken over from Wishart only recently. They quickly moved on thereafter to the main business of the meeting: the management buy-out offer by deSoutier.

Andrew Strain opened the discussion. 'I've had the opportunity to look at the proposal deSoutier's put before us in some detail since our last meeting. As you know, I'm a cautious man. And I have spent too long in Broadlands to want to see it go down the drain. I can't say I count deSoutier among my friends—I consider him too brash, and I never really approved of his initial appointment—but he has proved himself, or begun to, and from his figures it seems to me that the plan he's proposing is a sound one.

I note that he will be retaining the senior managers in his by-out proposals.'

'There are three executive directors,' Eileen O'Hara intervened, for Eric's benefit. 'Apart from deSoutier, Ralph Neilson and Jim Daly are also wishing to purchase shares in the leveraged buy-out.'

Andrew Strain looked sourly at her, annoyed by the interruption. 'Yes, well . . . in short, the retention of executive expertise makes the idea stronger in my view: it gives Broadlands a brighter future to have experience at the helm. I look favourably, therefore, upon his proposal. But that is, of course, before we hear from Hall Davies.'

There was a brief discussion in which Tom Black joined, lending his support to the comments made by Strain and stressing that for his part the future success of the company they had all worked for was as important as their getting a fair price for their shareholdings. 'But, like Andrew, I'm interested in hearing the result of Hall's discussions with Simon Wells.'

Hall Davies leaned forward, the index finger of his left hand caressing his thick moustache. 'Right, well, while I would have been in broad and general agreement with what Andrew and Tom are saying, I have to admit that the proposal that's come to us from Simon Wells and Consolidated Investments is an interesting one.'

'I don't like that man,' Andrew Strain murmured. 'He's an asset-stripping cowboy.'

'Pete Corsa isn't exactly everyone's cup of tea either,' Tom Black intervened, 'and he's backing deSoutier's bid.'

'Anyway,' Hall Davies went on, opening the manila folder in front of him, 'we must await a formal bid from Simon Wells, of course, but at this stage he's asked me to place an offer on the table to test reactions. As you'll all be aware, deSoutier has placed an offer before us which amounts to thirty million in total, a premium of some thirty per cent above the market price. I now have reason to believe that

Simon Wells will more than match that. In fact—' he paused, staring at the papers in front of him— 'it looks as though Mr Wells is prepared to put on the table an offer of thirty-four million. As part of the package, Neilson and Daly would be retained; deSoutier would not. The share price would be eighty pence.'

'Bloody hell!' Tom Black said quietly.

There was a short silence. Andrew Strain broke it. 'Thirty-four million. That's about fifteen per cent higher than the deSoutier offer.'

'You'll appreciate now,' Eileen O'Hara said calmly, 'why I did not invite Ted deSoutier and the other executive directors to this board meeting. Normally they would attend, of course,' she added, looking at Eric, 'for as executive directors they each hold a seat here. In the circumstances, considering a bid in which they have an interest, it was thought best to ask them to absent themselves.'

'Thirty-four million,' Tom Black repeated thoughtfully.

'Even if it's Simon Wells, we can't afford not to consider it,' Andrew Strain muttered.

'And we must also consider in what light this bid places the deSoutier offer,' Eileen O'Hara said.

The meeting lasted for almost two hours. It was remarkably low key in its discussion: the board members seemed vaguely alarmed by the Wells offer, as though they had taken a view of the company which had been underwritten by the deSoutier evaluation and which was now shattered by the new bid from Simon Wells. Andrew Strain voiced the doubts —did Wells really believe the company was worth the bid he was making, bearing in mind the market price of the shares quoted in the index? Or was this going to be a typical asset-stripping exercise, followed by a write-off of tax losses against his other company interests?

'It may even be based upon a desire to outdo Pete Corsa,' Tom Black suggested drily.

The discussion was inconclusive. What was clear was that while the board decided it needed more time, and supporting papers from Simon Wells, they were in some confusion of mind. When the meeting broke up they were served tea in the ante-room, and Eileen O'Hara took the opportunity to stand to one side with Eric.

'So, what do you think?' she asked.

'About the bids? Too early to say. But your board is in a buzz. They seem a bit overawed by the Wells intervention.'

'There's a lot of money on the table. Andrew Strain's wondering what Wells knows that he doesn't. Hall Davies is already half committed. Tom Black . . . well, I'm not sure about him.' She glanced at him, and there was a brooding, thoughtful glint in her eyes. 'He can be tough, devious . . . and charming. I know him well, but I've never got inside his head.'

The way she dwelled on her last words made Eric think she might have known Tom Black *very* well, in the past. He pushed the thought aside. 'What shareholdings do the executive directors have?'

'Qualification shares only—you know, just enough to make sure they have the kind of interest in the company that will give them the incentive to work at it. But it won't be enough to sway the vote at board level. They'll be clear enough what *they* want to do, of course: it's their bid, after all!'

'And you?' Eric asked.

Eileen O'Hara laughed. 'I'm confused too. But my confusion is overlaid with curiosity. I'm interested in discovering what Ted deSoutier's reaction might be. And,' she breathed, looking over Eric's shoulder and suddenly dropping her voice, 'it shouldn't be too long before we find out.'

Eric turned his head. A tall, dark-suited man was standing in the doorway. From the manner in which a sudden tension had descended, Eric could guess who he was.

The managing director of Broadlands had entered the room to join them at the conclusion of the board meeting.

3

Ted deSoutier was an impressive man. He wore his dark hair long, thrust back in a thick mane. He was as tall as Eric but more heavily built, with a tendency to corpulence that he might have difficulty in controlling in middle age. Now, in his late thirties, the energy that emanated from him would burn off any excess flesh; his eyes darted glances around the room constantly, as though he feared he would miss something, and there was a nervous tension about his movements that Eric guessed would be normal rather than induced by his clear and immediate desire to know how the board meeting might have gone on in his absence. His jawline was arrogant: he was used to getting his way. His mouth was hard and Eric imagined that swift decision-making came easily to him. He knew what he wanted now, and he knew where best to get it. He walked straight across the room towards Eileen O'Hara and Eric saw her straighten, almost unconsciously. She was aware of the power of deSoutier, in personal as well as professional terms.

'Hello, Ted.' Her tone was easy, in spite of the tension in her shoulders, as deSoutier stood squarely in front of her. 'Can I introduce you to Eric Ward? He's a lawyer; he's advising me.'

Ted deSoutier glanced at Eric, shook hands, summed him up in the handshake and allowed himself to be momentarily distracted from his main purpose in approaching Eileen O'Hara. 'Ward . . .' he repeated thoughtfully.

'The Salamander business,' O'Hara said sweetly, with a hint of provocation that was lost on Eric.

The managing director of Broadlands frowned, still staring at Eric, as though he was trying to determine what part a lawyer might be playing in the offer situation he had raised at Broadlands; then, perhaps characteristically, he swiftly dismissed the thought, turning back to O'Hara. He was not a man who would be easily swayed from a frontal attack. 'So what happened?' he demanded.

'At the board? No decision has been made as yet,' O'Hara replied.

'No decision? Are there questions being raised about our bid?'

Eileen O'Hara hesitated, slipped a quick glance towards Eric, and then said, 'No particular questions have been raised ... though I have a few which I haven't voiced yet.'

'What the hell's that supposed to mean?'

'Originally, the board was impressed by your bid, but in the circumstances ...'

There was a short silence as her words died away. Eric was aware that the rest of the room was uncomfortably silent: no one was looking in their direction, but there was no conversation being carried on over the teacups. DeSoutier's quick eyes were dangerously still for a few seconds as he stared at O'Hara. 'What ... circumstances?'

Eileen O'Hara put down her cup carefully on the table beside her. She looked straight at deSoutier. 'There's another bid come in ... a counter-offer.'

The silence grew around them. 'Higher?' deSoutier asked harshly, after several seconds.

'Considerably.'

'By how much?'

Eileen O'Hara hesitated, but Eric was left with the impression the hesitation was rooted not so much in uncertainty as in a desire to needle deSoutier. He stepped back slightly; he was aware of a certain electricity between these two, not explained by the situation. 'There's a difference of some fifteen per cent,' O'Hara said quietly. 'And that's why questions are being raised in my mind.'

The big man facing her did not pursue the thought. He

was angry, and was trying unsuccessfully to control his anger. 'This . . . offer you mention. Who's put it in?'

'I'm not certain it's ethical—'

'Stop this bloody pussyfooting, O'Hara!'

She paled, and her chin came up. It was now her turn to be provoked, by the contempt in his tone. 'The bid is a verbal one only,' she replied icily, 'and the board has made no decision as yet, nor has it seen any papers—'

'Who the hell's put it in?'

She flared. 'All right. You want to know. Let's make it public. The bid came from Simon Wells.'

Ted deSoutier stared at her and all his nervous energy suddenly seemed to be concentrated into his eyes. The first shock was replaced by fury, and when he spoke his voice was like gravel. 'You're not telling me the board is seriously going to consider a bid from that pirate.'

'He's bidding fifteen per cent higher than you are.'

'Which bloody well shows you it can't be anything other than some rip-off he has in mind. The shares aren't worth that kind of figure—'

'On *your* valuation, deSoutier, but is your valuation disinterested?' she flashed back. 'And in the end, the valuation will be based upon a market view, not the managing director's!'

'I know this company, and I'm telling you—'

'No, you're telling me nothing! Let's stay logical over this. You've put in a bid for a management buy-out. Fine. But now that the board is thinking about selling, there's another hat in the ring. You don't really believe we can just turn our backs on the offer?'

'There's a hell of a difference between me and Simon Wells!' deSoutier raged.

'I don't know Wells, so I can't draw the comparisons. But I tell you this, Ted, a bid fifteen per cent higher than yours makes me raise my eyebrows. And if you're in the mood for a shouting match, let's have one. I was nervous about your bid; I wasn't sure it was in the best interests of the company. But I was prepared to go along with it, give the issue the benefit of the doubt. Now, the Wells bid makes me pause: what is the true market valuation of Broadlands? I think we should try to find out.'

'You'd be throwing the company away to an asset-stripper if you sell out to Wells. Is that what you want?'

'I want to be in a situation where I can exercise an independent decision, rather than be browbeaten and bullied into one. You should know me better, Ted. This kind of argument can lead to only one point of view from me!'

'Eileen, I warn you—'

'Warn? Who the hell do you think you are?' She was now furious, but there were reasons behind her fury that Eric suspected were personal, and had little to do with the issue being debated between them. She stabbed the air with her forefinger in deSoutier's direction. 'Whatever uncertainties there might have been in my mind, it's damned certain now that they've been swept away. I'm going to vote for an open contest; I'm going to vote against acceptance of your buy-out!'

'You want to see me and Wells at each other's throats?'

'That's precisely it!'

The room was still. Tom Black was staring at her; Andrew Strain was pale. Only Hall Davies seemed detached, almost amused by the confrontation, a slight smile touching his lips.

Ted deSoutier took control of himself with a visible effort. He took a deep breath, unclenched his hands, nodding slowly at her words. 'All right, O'Hara, I hear you. I don't like what I hear, because it seems to me you're allowing personal animosities to intrude into what should be seen as a straight business decision. But maybe that's typical female hysteria.'

She tightened her lips; there was a quiver of fury in her shoulders, but she made no reply as he went on, obviously speaking for the benefit of the listening members of the board.

'I have always been under the impression that you were interested in the future of Broadlands as a company. It was one of the reasons why I was attracted to the job of managing director in the first place. And everything I've done since has been to develop and build the company—because I believed in it.' He paused, glancing around at the silent board members. 'And when Daly and Neilson and I put in our management buy-out proposal it was against that background. We believed in the company and still do; we want to turn it around. But now I hear you, O'Hara; I hear you're prepared to contemplate a bid from an arbitrageur whose only motive must be to make a fast buck. You and the board know how such people work! His tactics will be to push the share prices up by the threat of his bid, make a quick killing and get out—or else it'll be to take over the company, then strip it of its assets and leave the rest as a tax loss. Is that what the board wants for Broadlands? I wouldn't have thought so—but you seem to want it—and maybe for reasons that have nothing to do with the company and everything to do with me. Well, all I can say, O'Hara, is that if you want to play men's games you'd better expect to get bruised. If the board wants to look seriously at the Wells intervention, fine, but the gloves will then come off, I can assure you!'

Tom Black was moving forward, as though to intervene, calm things down. Eileen O'Hara spoke before he could. 'Taking the gloves off doesn't scare me, Ted—and I'm used to playing men's games.'

'When they turn serious?'

Her tone was cool. 'Just what do you have in mind?'

Tom Black was standing beside them, frowning. Ted deSoutier glared at him, detected the warning in his glance, and looked around the room at the other, silent directors of Broadlands. 'All right. I'll say no more. At least, not until the board decides exactly what it's going to do. But I heard you, O'Hara; I hope you heard me!'

He turned, and walked briskly away from them, out of the room. Eileen O'Hara glared after him, then turned to Tom Black. 'You should have let him have his say.'

The deputy chairman of Broadlands smiled quietly. 'I was thinking of you, Eileen. You were getting somewhat ... worked up.'

'Like a typical woman, is that it?' O'Hara sneered.

'I didn't say that.'

She stared at him coldly, then turned to the others. 'I think we should now reconvene. There's a resolution I wish to move from the chair.'

The silence around her as she walked back into the boardroom was icy.

Eric was puzzled. There had been something unreal about the confrontation between Eileen O'Hara and Ted deSoutier. No, on reflection, not unreal; rather it had been based upon matters that were not really related to the Simon Wells bid. The situation arising out of the conflicting bids had been used in some odd way, manipulated by both of them to bring out into the open an antagonism that had perhaps lain dormant for some time. Eric had been surprised at the venom in deSoutier's tones, and the deliberate remarks about her sex: he had been out to provoke a furious reaction—or else he had been paying off old scores.

The result had been swift. The reconvened board had been faced with a resolution from the chair that had been brief, and decisive. Eileen O'Hara had demanded that the board agree to receive a formal bid from Simon Wells.

It was Tom Black, reasonably, who had suggested they move a little more slowly and deliberately. O'Hara had rounded on her deputy chairman, still smarting from her confrontation with deSoutier, but he had stuck to his guns. Angrily, she had turned to Eric for advice.

'I would consider the best way to proceed,' Eric had suggested, 'would be for both parties now to be invited to make a further bid. Your managers have put in an offer; Wells has put in a counter-bid; the size of that bid is now known to deSoutier. I would therefore suggest that the interested parties be requested to enter sealed bids, to be received by a certain date: these bids should then be opened together. That would leave the board with a clear decision to make—and it would also, if publicized, allow the board to test the market potential of the company. We are all aware that once this kind of dispute hits the streets, speculation begins, but at least a view will be declared in the market place regarding the true value of Broadlands.'

It had been swiftly agreed thereafter.

Now, in the taxi that took Eric across town to the offices of Martin and Channing, there was the opportunity to consider again the nature of the confrontation between the managing director and chairman of Broadlands. The more he thought about it, the more Eric was convinced that the underlying issue was personal rather than professional, and not strictly connected with the business itself. O'Hara and deSoutier had crossed swords somewhere, but outside the confines of Broadlands. The thought gave Eric a certain unease which he found annoying: it was none of his business, he was employed to undertake a consultancy function, and this kind of extraneous probing into personal lives was outside his brief. Yet the thought kept straying into his mind, and he resented it. Eileen O'Hara was intruding too much into his mind for comfort.

Eric paid off the taxi outside the Martin and Channing building and made his way to the small office that had been set aside for his use during his infrequent visits to the merchant bank. There were some papers he had to deal with regarding the last board meeting, and he wanted to check on certain transactions agreed to by the board during one of his absences; he was on the board as a representative of Anne's interests and he felt it necessary to keep an eye on what Leonard Channing, in particular, got up to from time to time.

As he came out of the lift he almost collided with Leonard Channing, hurrying along the corridor towards the boardroom.

'Eric! Favouring us with your presence? Business must be bad on the Quayside!' Leonard Channing walked swiftly on, and then slowed, hesitated, glanced back over his shoulder. His voice was expressionless as he said, 'If you're not too busy, Eric, would you care to join me in my office in a few minutes? There's someone I'd like you to meet.'

Eric agreed, and entered his office, spent a few minutes sorting through the papers on his desk, and then went back along the corridor to join the chairman of Martin and Channing. Leonard called out as he knocked; Eric went in and a stocky, dark-haired man swung around in his chair, rising to his feet as Leonard called Eric in.

'Ah, Eric, I thought it might be useful if I were to introduce you to Mr Corsa. You'll have heard of him, of course, and of his investment bank.'

Eric had certainly heard of Pete Corsa and of his investment bank. The man was not what he had expected, physically, however. Corsa was perhaps five feet eight in height, heavily built, swarthy complexioned. There was an almost Sicilian cast to his features but his eyes were a piercing blue. His lips were fleshy, he was carrying more weight than would have been comfortable, and his dark hair was tightly curled, almost effeminate in its styling. When he shook hands his flesh felt soft, but his grip was strong. Eric had the feeling it would be a reflection of his character: seemingly soft and weak, there was nevertheless an underlying ruthlessness that would have explained his position and reputation in the financial world. Corsa's investment bank was a successful one, and the man himself rarely seemed to be on the losing side in any financial situation. There had been rumours of overstretching of recent years but nothing concrete, and Corsa was still seen as an important shark in the red financial seas. The stains had rarely been caused by his own hæmorrhaging.

'I'm pleased to meet you, Mr Corsa.'

'Mr Ward.' The investment banker looked up at Eric, a half-smile on his thick lips. 'I understand we're sort of working in the same field at the moment.'

Eric glanced warily towards Leonard Channing. The man's narrow, cunning face projected a false innocence; he spread his hands in protestation. 'We've just been talking about financial matters, Eric. Mr Corsa wanted to see me to discuss the raising of certain sums to support a market bid, and in the course of conversation it came out the bid related to Broadlands. I immediately considered it would be useful if you met, in view of your own position.'

The stress upon the word 'position' was not lost upon Corsa. The banker looked quizzically at Eric. 'You have some connection with Broadlands?'

'I have.'

'The fact is,' Leonard announced cheerfully,' Mr Corsa wanted to talk to me about Martin and Channing taking what our American friends call a slice of the action in the bid for Broadlands.'

'The bid?' Eric asked non-committally.

Corsa watched him carefully. 'There's been a management buy-out proposal for control of Broadlands. My bank is supporting that bid: I've guaranteed a twelve million support fund for the leveraged buy-out. Naturally, I'm more than happy to lay off some of that fund into a stake for other banking houses: I thought maybe Martin and Channing would be interested. But what's your involvement?'

'A difficult one,' Eric said shortly. 'I'm advising Miss O'Hara.'

'On the bid? It's a straightforward one.'

'Not so straightforward,' Eric replied.

Leonard Channing smiled wolfishly. 'You've just come back from a board meeting, Eric? Is there anything to report?'

Eric suppressed the anger stirring in his veins. He knew Channing was needling him, and he was unwilling to rise to the bait. 'I have obligations to Miss O'Hara . . .'

'And to this bank, surely,' Channing protested mockingly. 'I mean, if there is information you think we should have in any of our dealings, surely you owe us a duty to disclose—'

'In this matter, you'll have to concede that my duty lies to Broadlands,' Eric insisted stubbornly,' and I can hardly be expected to disclose information I might have received at the Broadlands board—'

'Not even if it affects Martin and Channing?'

'I don't see how it can affect Martin and Channing—'

'When I'm entering negotiations with Mr Corsa for a stake in the management buy-out? Tell me, Eric, if there is information from Broadlands which might affect my decision to work with Mr Corsa, would you tell me of it?'

'It depends.'

'There speaks a lawyer,' Channing sighed theatrically, clearly enjoying himself. 'Mr Corsa, there lies the problem. Eric can never be sure exactly where his loyalty lies! A clash of interests, wouldn't you say?'

Corsa was fully aware a cat and mouse game was being played. He was interested, nevertheless—not in Channing's provocative challenges, but in what might underlie them. He fixed Eric with a calculating glance. 'You suggest the . . . management buy-out isn't exactly all that simple. I gather from that the Broadlands board might not have accepted the bid.'

Eric stared at him, irritated by Leonard Channing's subterfuges. This meeting had been arranged deliberately, even if on the spur of the moment. The objective was clear:

Leonard Channing wished to embarrass Eric. He glanced at his watch. The board meeting had been over for an hour. An announcement would inevitably appear in the evening press. There was little point in not allowing Leonard his little triumph. 'I . . . I'm not saying the board will or will not accept the bid.'

Corsa was no fool. He sighed. 'They haven't yet accepted it then.'

'Possibly,' Leonard Channing purred, 'the newspaper speculation at the weekend hasn't been too far off the mark. Perhaps the board is undecided because another bid is in?'

Corsa looked at Eric and raised his eyebrows. Eric nodded. 'Another verbal bid has been placed,' he confirmed.

'Interesting,' Leonard Channing breathed pleasurably. 'Now that *is* useful, Eric. It's nice to know you're prepared to show your loyalty to Martin and Channing when delicate situations arise. Even if it does mean perhaps a little . . . disloyalty to your consultancy . . .'

'The notice will be in the financial press this evening,' Eric said shortly.

'And the name of the bidder?' Corsa asked.

'Yes,' Eric replied, without offering the information.

Leonard Channing chuckled. 'Ah, you see the dilemma our young friend finds himself in, Mr Corsa. Indeed, he finds himself in such a situation often, because he will insist on having a finger in so many pies. As if his villainous practice on Tyneside were not enough . . . However, I'm pleased I did call Eric in, because it demonstrates that further discussions between us, Mr Corsa, should perhaps await further disclosures regarding the Broadlands board decision. Clearly, while Martin and Channing are interested in joining forces to support the LBO fund you talked of, a decision on the matter can only be taken in the light of what other bids might emerge. We would not wish to commit ourselves to an open-ended battle for a shareholding where the prices could rise automatically, as they often do in power struggles of the kind that might now develop.'

'I can see that, Channing. However, I'd like to go over certain details with you—'

'Of course, of course, my dear chap. Eric, we needn't detain you longer . . .'

Corsa rose, and shook hands with Eric again. His eyes were careful, appraising. 'I trust we'll meet again, Ward.'

Eric left and made his way back to his office. He felt a cold anger in his veins. He went through the papers on his desk but was barely aware of their contents. He knew what was coming.

Half an hour later the phone rang. It was Leonard Channing.

'Eric? Just a word. You'll appreciate my . . . *our* position.'

'There is no conflict of interest, Leonard.'

'Not yet, dear boy, not yet. But you see, there could be. I mean, what if I were to enter a deal with Corsa, to your knowledge, and you were holding information from Broadlands that might have affected my decision . . . but which you did not—'

'*Could* not.'

'—divulge? Precisely. You see my point. Clash of loyalty; conflict of interest.'

'It doesn't arise.'

'No?' There was a short silence. Eric could hear Channing's breathing, easy, leisured, self-satisfied. 'I've had a call from Simon Wells. You know, the arbitrageur. He wants to see me.'

'Yes?'

'It's about a management buy-out.'

'So?'

'I wonder why Martin and Channing are becoming so wanted, suddenly? Is it because certain people know of your advisory situation with Broadlands and think that we might be able to . . . help?'

'Leonard—'

'I wouldn't want this bank to get involved in any form of insider dealing, Eric.'

'There's nothing I—'

'Of course, where there's a conflict of interest, and loyalty, it's always easy to resolve the matter by a resignation from one position or the other. You know, relinquish the advisory thing with Broadlands . . . or resign from the board of Martin and Channing.'

Eric was silent. Channing had got to the matter more quickly than he would have expected. 'At this stage, Leonard, there is no conflict of interest,' he repeated.

'My dear boy, essentially, I agree with you. But I thought it best to have the conversation, as a matter of record. Just to make sure, however: if I do talk with Wells, or Corsa, and am near decision, you will be kind enough to keep me informed of relevant matters that might affect the decision, won't you? And I can feel confident that you'll undertake nothing that might bring Martin and Channing into disrepute in the City, can't I?'

Channing rang off, awaiting no reply to his semi-rhetorical question. Sourly, Eric replaced the phone on its cradle. He knew exactly what was in Leonard Channing's mind. Eric Ward was to be encouraged to continue with the Broadlands consultancy. The encouragement lay in Leonard's understated warning: he knew his man, knew Eric would react stubbornly, insisting on continuing to work for Eileen O'Hara merely because of the warning.

But at the same time Leonard would be hoping for a clash of interest, and a failure on Eric's part to warn the Martin and Channing chairman of 'relevant' facts. Eric knew that Channing would now almost certainly throw in his lot with either Corsa or Wells. In the hope that eventually, it might lead to a call for the resignation of Eric Ward from the board of Martin and Channing. The tightrope had been erected. Eric was now being gently prodded along it.

And the ringmaster, Leonard Channing, was eagerly waiting for him to fall.

CHAPTER 3

1

'The curlews are early this year.'

On the hill a tractor was droning across the fields, spreading the first silage, and above it wheeled a pair of curlew, their plaintive piping call echoing across the bare fell and down to the meadow. For Eric the birds were always the first intimation of spring; they had wintered, feeding in the bays and estuaries but were now coming inland to the high fells to nest. For him the high country would not be the same without their sad call and as he stood beside Anne on the terrace he felt the old, deep satisfaction he always experienced at Sedleigh when the curlew returned.

'I'm sorry I didn't get back in time to see you last night,' Anne said, sipping the mug of steaming coffee she held. 'By the time I'd flown in to Newcastle, I couldn't face the drive to Sedleigh so I stayed at the flat, so I could make an early start this morning. I was on the road by six.'

'I didn't get back until quite late myself,' Eric remarked. 'I thought I'd better clear a few things at the Quayside first; if I'd realized you'd be staying at the flat I'd have hung on.'

'We really ought to communicate more.'

Eric looked at her. She kept her face averted, eyes screwed against the morning sunshine as she looked up to the hill. He could not be sure, but he felt he detected an underlying irony in the remark: it had not been completely casual.

'How did Stavanger go?'

'Well enough,' she replied. 'The timber deal looks like going through. But I had an odd call while I was there. From Leonard Channing.'

'Yes?'

She still did not look at him. 'You know what Leonard is like. The first chance to get a knife in, he does. But what he was saying this time made me wonder whether the knife is going to dig more deeply than usual.'

'What *was* he saying?'

She sipped her coffee. 'In brief, he felt he was in a dilemma. He's been approached by two competing investment houses—the Melling Investment Bank—'

'Pete Corsa.'

'And Simon Wells.'

'I knew about it.'

'He thought he should tell me, because in his view there's the possibility of a conflict of interest situation, involving you as a member of the Martin and Channing board, because of your . . . relationship with Broadlands.'

'There isn't . . . but he suggests it would be a good thing if I resigned from the board?'

She flicked a quick glance at Eric, and shook her head. 'He didn't say that exactly. He considered the situation might worsen, and it was as well I should know. As a sort of forewarning.'

'I can believe that,' Eric said drily.

She was silent for a few moments. 'He did suggest that the matter could be resolved by your being replaced on the board of Martin and Channing.'

'It's your nomination, Anne. I'm just there as your representative. If you feel I should be replaced, it's entirely up to you.'

'You make it sound like a vote of confidence in you,' she said quickly.

'I don't mean to. I merely state the facts. As Leonard

would expect me to. He's out to make trouble—you know that as well as I do. He always saw me as a tame goose on the board—a figurehead for you who would keep his mouth shut. It's not been that way, and he's unhappy. But in this case he might have a point. And the situation is certainly as I outlined—the seat on the board lies in your power, not mine.'

'There is another option.'

'That's right.' He moved, to sit on the terrace wall so that he was facing her directly. He knew the alternative course she had in mind; resignation from his consultancy with Broadlands. Maybe, *maybe* it was a step he should take to avoid professional problems and marital conflict. It was a step he was unwilling to take because in his view it would be an admission of defeat, an acceptance of pressure that was not based on rational argument. He waited for Anne to propose it, but she had more sense. She met his glance steadily, saying nothing. 'So?' he asked.

'I certainly don't wish to sit on the board of Martin and Channing myself,' she said slowly. 'I have enough on my plate with Morcomb Estates, and besides, I know nothing about the City. Although I could get . . . someone else, I suppose, a lawyer like you . . .'

Eric waited.

She shrugged. 'But there seems little point at this stage. Leonard's smoothing his way along in his usual snaky way, causing trouble, but there's no real issue on the table yet, is there?'

'Not yet,' Eric agreed gravely.

'So let's leave it. For the moment.' She sighed. 'I've plenty else to worry about anyway.'

'I thought you said Stavanger went well.'

'Not Stavanger. The Eddie Paulson business.'

'Ah.' The collapse of the Amble marina building contracts. They were on dangerous ground again, discussing Paulson. It was odd how the two issues seemed to weave and interlink one with another. Anne's displeasure regarding his relationship with Broadlands seemed never far from his own dissatisfaction over her retaining the charlatan lawyer Davison to handle the Paulson affair. 'So what's the latest state of play?'

'I instructed Davison, as you know,' Anne said in a slightly defensive tone. 'He's had a series of meetings, with Paulson and his advisers. It's clear that Paulson does *not* want litigation.'

'Obviously. But neither do you, if you can avoid it.'

'We've had confirmation that the loss is likely to be around the four million mark.'

'As you suspected. Has Davison managed to screw any admissions out of Paulson?'

'Not really, and Paulson is still insisting that the real liability lies elsewhere, with his suppliers and all that sort of thing. He's wriggling like hell.'

'But is prepared to settle out of court?'

Anne finished her coffee and put the mug down. She put her hands on her hips, breathed deeply. He could see the line of her breasts lift, and he was aware suddenly that it was well over a week since they had been together like this, and close. 'Well, he has told Davison, without prejudice, that he'd be prepared to settle for two million. But it's not negotiable.'

'Settle.'

She stared at him, surprised at his decisiveness. 'Just like that? Are you serious? To settle for that would be . . . it would be like throwing my hand in! I thought you would have advised me to fight.'

'What's Davison's view?'

'Like you, he says go for it. But damn it, that means writing off two million pounds!'

'Not really. Like it or not, Morcomb Estates is in a spot. You're four million adrift. You can haul back two, without further action. There are insurances cover you can make claims against. You can cut back that loss significantly. But if Paulson is serious about no negotiation—and it's likely, because two million is probably all he can afford—any further pressure from Morcomb Estates could lead to his bankruptcy, the costs of a suit . . . I tell you, darling, don't give it all to the lawyers, take the money on the table, put it down to experience, and run.'

'And count our losses!'

'Loss is inevitable. It's a matter of minimizing that loss.'

'You sound like Davison.'

'I regret that.'

She looked at him angrily for a moment, and then her lips twitched and she laughed, drawn away from her gloominess over the Paulson business. 'He's doing a good job.'

'Maybe he's reformed.'

'Maybe you were wrong.'

'All things are possible.'

She paused, raised her chin to look at him levelly. 'Such as my seeing a bit more of you in the next few weeks?'

The atmosphere between them had suddenly changed, the tension replaced by a shiver of knowledge and expectation. Eric stood up away from the wall and held out his hand. Anne took it, and he drew her towards him. Their thighs touched and her arms slid around his neck. 'I now certainly regret not getting back last night,' she murmured.

'Mornings can be good.'

'Sometimes, even better.'

He kissed her, and felt her body move against his. Her skin was soft under his fingertips, and he felt the quickening of her heartbeat. As he held her close there was a murmur deep in her throat, a growing urgency in her body. After a little while she drew away from him and smiled, before turning to go indoors.

Eric looked about him. Above the meadow he caught sight of a kestrel, hovering, almost motionless in the still morning air, watching, waiting for the moment of the kill. It reminded him of Leonard Channing.

It was the wrong time for such reflections. He dismissed the thought and went inside, where Anne was waiting.

2

The early part of the following week was spent in Newcastle at the Quayside office. A number of files were awaiting him, most importantly a complex speed and performance clause in a five year time charterparty on the New York Produce Exchange Form. While Eric's practice was growing on the marine side there were yet specialist areas where he could not hope to deal with the issues directly. It meant yet another visit to London, to take counsel's opinion, after several phone calls.

The Queen's Counsel, an Inner Temple man called Standcross, saw Eric in his chambers at Temple Gardens and dealt speedily with the matter as though he wished to emphasize the superiority of his intellect and experience.

'Well, Mr Ward, as I see it the clause provides there shall be an equitable reduction of hire if the vessel fails to meet her guaranteed average speed and fuel consumption.'

'That's right.'

'The clause further provides that the hire shall be increased in the event that the vessel betters the stipulated performance.'

'Correct.'

'Your client claims an increased hire on the basis that the vessel in question did exceed the requirements. The other side argues that the clause was uncertain in its interpretation.'

'That is the dispute, yes.'

The QC pressed the tips of his fingers together and looked at Eric over his glasses. 'Your client is fortunate. I've just got back from the States. I was acting for a client in an issue very similar to this. Arrangements with the New York Bar and England have been concluded and opinions are in line. A clause of this kind is now regarded as sufficiently certain to give your client a right to claim. He can be rewarded with an increase in hire, in the same way that the other side would have been able to claim a reduction, in the appropriate circumstances. I would refer you to the Atlantic Lines and Navigation case of 1987. It's reported in Lloyd's Reports. I'll write out a full opinion, of course. But you should have no difficulty. A glass of sherry, Mr Ward?'

Somewhat taken aback, Eric admitted he never drank sherry.

Standcross smiled. 'Good, prefer whisky myself.' He rose from behind his desk and walked across the room to the glass-fronted rosewood cabinet in the corner. He selected two glasses, and poured a small measure in each. 'Glenfiddich.'

Eric thought it would be churlish to refuse.

'Here's to the continued existence of the two branches of the profession,' the barrister toasted.

'And confusion to the Lord Chancellor?'

The QC smiled. 'Ah. Law Reform. That's what comes of having a Scotsman appointed as Lord Chancellor. Dammit, he was trained in Roman Law, not the English Common Law! However, no more of that. You're not often in the Temple, Ward.'

'That's right. My practice rarely calls for counsel's opinion. I deal in small beer.'

'Except in the City, as I understand it. Your name came up recently, at a small dinner-party I was attending.'

'Oh?'

'Talk turned to the Salamander affair. It seems the story is you were quite . . . central to it.'

'The part I played has been exaggerated.'

Standcross eyed him carefully, and sipped his whisky. 'Possibly, but I think not. However, I was interested to meet you this morning. Not least because my host that evening had mentioned your name. Indeed, he went rather further than mentioning your name. He said he'd like to meet you. I agreed to raise the matter with you.'

Eric smiled, somewhat puzzled. 'I don't think that I'm particularly inaccessible. A phone call—'

Leather creaked as the QC shifted in his seat. 'You must understand, I find myself in a difficult situation. A friend . . . we were at Cambridge together, you know . . . I saw no harm in raising the matter with you—at his request—'

'What matter?'

'A meeting here.'

'At your chambers?'

'He'll be here in about ten minutes. I have to go to a consultation shortly, so if it is not inconvenient for you . . .'

Eric frowned, then managed a laugh. 'This is a little . . . cloak and dagger, isn't it? A Queen's Counsel, acting as a go-between—'

'Not quite that,' Standcross said stiffly. 'A favour, for an old friend. But if it is inconvenient . . .'

'No, I didn't say that. But who is this friend of yours?'

The QC finished his whisky in a quick gulp. He looked at his watch. 'I really must go . . . If you'd care to wait, my clerk will see to any of your requirements. As for my friend, he is active in the City. You'll have heard of him. He's called Simon Wells.'

Standcross's chambers overlooked the Inner Temple gardens. The chambers were what he would describe as commodious and well-appointed, as befitted his station. But Standcross would never dominate them as Simon Wells appeared to do. The arbitrageur seemed to fill the room. He was over six feet in height but it was not his size that impressed as much as the energy he seemed to emanate. He was perhaps forty years of age, lean, with almost effeminate hands, but his eyes were sharp, his voice deep and incisive and his manner peremptory. He was clearly used to swiftness in decision-making and it was reflected in a certain restlessness of movement; after introducing himself to Eric he did not sit down but moved around the room, pacing it in an almost feline way, prowling, as he sought the right phrases to use. He had thinning red hair, grey at the temples, and pale eyelashes; he was immaculately suited, and a single ring gleamed on his left hand as a concession to flamboyancy. He raised in Eric a feeling of wariness; it was communicated to Wells, who smiled thinly.

'You find this an unusual method of introduction, Mr Ward.'

'I do.'

'A matter of convenience only. Your name came up, I made use of an old acquaintance.'

Simon Wells would always make use of acquaintances, Eric considered.

'There's also the matter of the City,' Wells continued. 'It's very like a small village. Everyone knows what everyone else is doing. Or wants to know. Part of my success has been based on the fact that I keep my intentions to myself. Until the right time comes.'

'And by meeting like this, through an intermediary unconnected with the City—'

'No one makes the connection.'

'I'm not certain what the connection is . . . or should be,' Eric said quietly.

Simon Wells stabbed at the air with a dismissive hand. 'The connection must be obvious. Broadlands.'

Eric was silent for a moment. Then he rose to his feet and walked to the window. The trees in the Inner Temple garden were just beginning to show leaf; traffic roaring past on the Embankment produced only a muted sound across the green of the gardens. Two gowned barristers were in conversation in the square. A tug hooted on the river. 'I don't think I can help you, Mr Wells.'

'Before you even know what I want?'

'I think I know what you want. You're aware I'm on the board of Martin and Channing. You know I'm retained as an adviser by Broadlands, in the management buy-out proposal. And you know also that the Melling Investment Bank and Pete Corsa is behind the deSoutier bid. What you want from me, I guess, is any information I can give you about that bid —now that sealed tenders are being asked for.'

Simon Wells snorted contemptuously. 'Information? If I want information it's not *you* I'd come to, Ward. You're an innocent in this jungle. My sealed bid will go in and match anything that Corsa and deSoutier can raise. And if I wanted to buy you, as you seem to think, I'd be a bloody sight more subtle than this, believe me. Besides, the story is that you're one of those curious characters it's difficult to suborn or corrupt.'

'Only *difficult?*' Eric asked.

'Everyone has a price. Haven't you heard that? But I'm not seeking to find what your price is. I don't want information from you. I want to *give* you information.'

Eric stared at him, puzzled. 'I don't understand.'

'I want to get Pete Corsa. You need to know that.'

'Why?'

'Because it emphasizes that the price as far as I'm concerned is irrelevant. And as an adviser to Eileen O'Hara that's something you need to know.'

Behind the pale eyelashes the man's eyes were cold. Eric shook his head. 'You mean you're prepared to pay over the odds just to stop deSoutier's management buy-out being successful?'

'I've nothing against deSoutier. But Corsa is a guy I intend stopping.'

It was none of Eric's business, but he asked, nevertheless. 'Why?'

Simon Wells prowled the room restlessly. 'I could go back over the years. I could mention a number of situations: the

Maxton Corporation takeover, the Springfield merger . . . no matter, they're not important now. Besides, that's business. You win a few, you lose a few. Broadlands is different.'

'How?'

Wells grunted. 'You have to look at the City ever since Big Bang. Things have changed. And the shakeout during the last couple of years has shifted the goalposts as well. It's meant that in some areas business has declined. I'm an arbitrageur, sure; but I'm not unlike Pete Corsa in that I have to look out for new business if it isn't rushing through the door. So, two years ago, I did the rounds of the corporate chief executives. I put certain proposals to them. A selected few looked to come good. Ted deSoutier was one of them. The fact is, I put together a financial package for a Broadlands buy-out well before Pete Corsa came on the scene.'

'I see.'

'Do you? Maybe, maybe not. I'm a reasonable guy. Things went quiet. I wasn't in touch with deSoutier: I had other irons in the fire. And then, suddenly, I hear that deSoutier's done a deal with someone I regard as a rival. Pete Corsa and the Melling Investment Bank. That makes me angry. It was *I* who set up that programme. So I went to deSoutier but he just referred me to Corsa. It seemed right to me, having done the groundwork, that I ought to get a cut, a slice of the action. But there was no way I'd go cap in hand to Corsa. He'd have just told me to go to hell, anyway—as in similar circumstances I'd have told him. That's when I decided I'd put in my own bid. That's why I approached Hall Davies. That's why my hat's in the ring.'

'Irrespective of the value of Broadlands?'

Wells smiled thinly. 'Don't get me wrong. Broadlands is a sound acquisition. I want it, through the managers. With the exception of deSoutier, of course. On the other hand, I would not be entirely dissatisfied if I pushed Corsa further than he would want to go.'

Eric watched the big man for a few moments, thinking. 'It seems to me,' he said slowly, 'there's an element of irrationality in your attitude. I can understand you see Corsa as a rival; I can understand you might want to make him bleed for disrupting a deal you might have struck with deSoutier. But it seems . . . an overreaction . . .'

Wells's pale eyelashes were lowered. He looked at his hands, spread his fingers thoughtfully. 'Maybe you're right, Ward. It could look a bit over the top. But then, although you may be active in the City, it's clear you haven't tuned into the village yet. The gossip hasn't got to you.'

'Gossip?'

Wells stared at him coldly. 'There's more than one reason why I would want to see Pete Corsa eat dirt.' He grimaced suddenly, as though bitterness had touched his tongue. 'Anyway, you get the message, I guess. You can tell your client that my bid will be in—and you can tell her I'm deadly serious.'

'I'll pass the message on,' Eric replied soberly.

They left Standcross's chambers together, but separated outside, Wells walking towards Holborn, Eric heading for the Embankment, and a stroll along the river wall with the opportunity to mull over what Simon Wells had said.

The auction decision was announced the next day in the press: Broadlands was the subject of discussion in the financial columns, the management buy-out proposal being dissected, and the news that the arbitrageur Wells was also in the running causing certain speculative pieces to appear. Eric had stayed overnight at his club, since he had a board meeting of Martin and Channing to attend. The meeting was over in the early afternoon, Leonard Channing keeping business discussion to a minimum and making no reference to Eric's situation with regard to Eileen O'Hara, although he did announce at the board that he had entered discussions with Pete Corsa about support for the Broadlands management buy-out.

There was a flight from Heathrow back north at seven in the evening; Eric had plenty of time to catch the plane, so when he was handed a message on leaving the offices of Martin and Channing, he was not averse to taking up the suggestion in the note.

'If you've time for a drink, could we meet? Give me a ring at the office.'

The signature was Phil Cooper's. Eric was curious enough to make the call.

They met in the lounge bar of a pub in Fleet Street. The deregulation of opening hours, a few years earlier, would have meant a crowded bar with a considerable number of journalists present; now, with Fleet Street losing its pre-eminent position in the printing world the bar was half empty, with a weary look, and journalists were noticeable by their absence.

When the financial journalist came in he was very noticeable. He was a big, square-built man who seemed to strain to get out of his suit. His shoulders threatened to burst from his jacket; his chunky features were split with a friendly grin and his grip, when he shook hands, was powerful. He could take on the appearance of a buffoon, and Eric felt he occasionally cultivated an untidiness of dress and a deliberate insouciance that was really designed to disarm calculation. But he would never be able to disguise the piercing shrewdness of his ice-blue eyes, and Eric was aware that Cooper had not sought him out for the pleasure of his company.

'What are you drinking?' the big man asked as he slid on to a bar stool.

'I've got something. Let me buy you one.'

'Half a bitter will do fine.'

'A financial journalist, drinking mere bitter?'

'Underrated, and underpaid,' Cooper grunted. 'Not like you City lawyers. So what's the news, then?'

'About what?'

Cooper waited until his drink was served. Then he raised the glass, toasting Eric silently. 'Broadlands, of course.' When he saw Eric's hesitation, he smiled. 'Come on, you knew perfectly well I'd want to see you to pump you about the bid situation.'

'There's little or nothing I can tell.'

'But you came.'

Eric nodded. He hesitated. 'That's right. You know the City.'

'And you want something from me . . . in return for which . . .?'

Eric shrugged. 'I'm prepared to keep you informed . . . as long as that doesn't break any confidences I have with my client.'

'O'Hara.' Cooper grimaced. 'Tough lady, that. She bedded you yet?' He caught the gleam in Eric's eye and raised his hand. 'OK, out of order, it just slipped out. But she's single, and available, so the story goes . . . she has a bit of a tigerish reputation, though I have to admit it's only gossip—'

'You pick up City gossip,' Eric said flatly.

'It's not my job,' Cooper replied. He eyed Eric shrewdly. 'But I pick up snippets here and there. But don't tell me you want gossip on your client, O'Hara.'

For a moment Eric thought back to Eileen O'Hara and her confrontation with deSoutier. He was tempted to ask Cooper whether there had been any rumours of a relationship between O'Hara and deSoutier, but resisted it. He shook his head. 'No. I'm rather more interested in Simon Wells.'

Cooper downed his drink and ordered another, with an orange juice for Eric. 'Wells, hey? Interesting. Our ships meet then. The reason why I wanted to see you was to get some solid information on a Wells bid. Rumour suggests he'll be coming in hard.'

'It looks like it.'

'*Real* hard?' Cooper pressed.

Eric shrugged. 'The auction has been announced. The Melling Investment Bank is backing deSoutier in his buy-out proposal. Wells will certainly be putting a package together. And it seems that . . . well, it will be a considerable package.'

Cooper nodded thoughtfully. 'I wondered . . . Have you seen the lunch-time Stock Exchange prices?'

'No.'

'Broadlands is pushing up fast.'

'Not surprising.'

'Maybe so. But I mean, very fast. There's a rumour that this is going to be a real fight—nastier than one would normally expect. I just wondered whether you might have some information that would . . . well, you know . . .'

'Tell me about Simon Wells,' Eric interrupted. 'And Pete Corsa.'

'Corsa? Well, they're rivals, of course, and if one can put the knife in the other, he will, but . . .' Cooper paused, his ice-blue eyes narrowing as he stared at Eric. 'But you're not suggesting there's personal needle coming into this, are you?'

'I'm asking, not suggesting.'

'Bloody hell,' Phil Cooper breathed. 'Now *that's* a new one! Wells turning human!'

'I don't understand.'

'I can't say I do, entirely.' Cooper shook his chunky head. 'I mean, this is *business*! But if I guess right, from your question . . . are you really saying that Wells is going seriously for Corsa?'

'My understanding,' Eric said carefully, 'is that Wells is prepared to go . . . beyond the true value of Broadlands to nail Corsa.'

'Now that *is* interesting.'

'But why should he be so committed?'

'Business is business, and there's the chance to do down a rival finance wheeler-dealer?'

"No."

Cooper managed a grin. 'No. You won't buy that one.' He paused, staring at his drink, and shook his head again. 'Who would have thought it . . .? You see, Ward, Wells has the reputation of being a cold fish. A piranha. Or a snake. A cobra. You choose. But any way you look, he's committed, cold as ice, ready to sell his grandmother . . . or his wife. And now, suddenly, it seems he is actually human.'

'You need to be more specific,' Eric suggested.

'You want the gossip.' Cooper nodded. 'OK, you've given me something; I'll give you the return. What I know about it, anyway.'

'Simon Wells?'

'Ahuh. I told you, he's a cold fish, with a tough reputation. But the guy's no different, they say, in his private life. You don't see him night-clubbing, but he gets around. A number of very wealthy and very beautiful women have had their names linked with his.'

'He's a womanizer?'

'Not exactly,' Cooper demurred. 'He likes women—if they're wealthy. And the relationships have been short-lived. It's as though the combination—looks and money—turns him on. I suppose for some people, money can be an aphrodisiac. Maybe he needs the combination. But the story is, that's his inclination—but few of them achieved more than one night stands with him. Until Ilse.'

'Who?'

'He got married.' Cooper shrugged. 'She was Scandinavian. Old money. The marriage was quick—and a surprise to the City. It was no surprise when it didn't last long.'

'So what happened?' Eric asked.

'No one can say for sure. But there's gossip . . . The facts are that she slipped up, with another guy. Some rumours suggest that our calculating friend Wells actually set the liaison up, for his own purposes—used her to get inside financial information. There's one school of thought that it must have been that way—I mean, look at Wells. What woman would leave *him* for the squat, Sicilian type?'

Eric frowned. 'The gossip—'

'She was typical picturebook Nordic, you know? Tall, slim, but a good figure, classical features, short blonde hair —elegant. Beddable, certainly, but maybe Wells saw her as a business asset. Maybe he did use her. Even so, to push her into Corsa's bed—'

'*Who?*'

Cooper stared at him, and grunted. 'That's the story, my friend. Pete Corsa cuckolded Wells; or Wells used his wife to get an edge on Corsa in some deal or other. Take your choice. Either way, it went sour. Ilse left Wells, stayed with Corsa a while, then went back to Norway. And then . . . maybe it was the long winters. Or maybe it's just that these Nordic types are just naturally gloomy. Anyway, a month ago she took an overdose.'

'She killed herself?'

'That's about it.' Cooper shrugged. 'Who knows why? For a broken marriage? For Corsa bedding her and then dumping her? For the young stallions she shacked up with these last eight months in Norway? Who knows? And as far as the City is concerned, who cares?'

Eric was silent for a little while. 'It seems,' he suggested quietly, 'that maybe Simon Wells cares.'

Phil Cooper finished his drink. 'And that's what makes things suddenly very interesting. It seems he's human after all. And in the kind of business Wells is in, human emotions can be very dangerous attributes.'

'How do you mean?'

'The City tries to work on a rational basis. All right, it panics regularly, with every shift in the financial wind. But it does try, and it rationalizes its behaviour. The finance world plays percentages. Mavericks cause trouble: they don't go by the rules. Pete Corsa knows the rules: he knows when to back off. Wells has always been the same. But now, suddenly, it seems things are different. Our arbitraging friend is telling us he's got a human streak after all. Ilse is dead, and he's after Pete Corsa. There's no percentage in it for him, financially, but he's going for Corsa's financial jugular. In a situation like that, all hell can break loose in the City.'

The big man slid off the bar stool and shook his head thoughtfully. 'Well, let's keep in touch, Ward. If there's any way I can help, you know my number. In return, I'd be grateful for the occasional chat—keep my finger on the pulse.'

'We'll do that.'

'OK, so I'll be seeing you. Meanwhile, keep an eye on the weather.'

'The weather? Why?'

Phil Cooper grinned sourly, and turned for the door. 'It could soon be raining blood.'

CHAPTER 4

1

Eric did not find it easy to concentrate on business in hand at the Quayside office during the following weeks. There was certainly enough to get on with: there was the defence of a client who had used his position to place an order for inferior steel for his firm, in return for which he had got his house rewired by the contractor. It was a petty piece of corruption, but when questioning his client Eric discovered that the contractor was not averse to regular bribery of this kind, and that there was a significant number of similar offences in the background. The police and the tax investigators visited him, and he was forced to spend a great deal of time on the issues arising. And then there was Garrity.

The request for representation came through from Garrity's employers as the Irish track addict had predicted, and Eric was as good as his word, but when the papers arrived from Donald Enderby, the solicitor acting for the other side, it soon became apparent that the case against Garrity—and consequently his employers on the ground of vicarious liability—as well founded and not difficult to prove. The County Court judge before whom they appeared was equally clear about the liability, from the manner in which he huffed and puffed impatiently while Enderby presented his case. He clearly felt it was all so obvious as not to merit long-winded speeches.

'In summary,' Enderby argued, 'when the telephone records are checked against the times when Garrity was present at the offices in question, there can be little doubt that the commitments of £1400 were in fact incurred by Garrity. I would then refer once again to the contract which Garrity's employers had entered into with the firms themselves. Clause fourteen is strictly drawn and is quite clear in its construction. That clause provides that the cleaning firm is to be regarded as strictly liable for all acts undertaken by their employees while they are on the premises of the plaintiffs. It is on that basis, and that clause, that compensation is sought from the employers for the sum expended by Garrity in his phone calls to the racetrack.'

The judge was clearly of the same opinion. Eric forestalled him. 'While the actions of Garrity can hardly be in dispute I still wish to take issue on the matter of vicarious liability.'

'You wish to raise arguments, Mr Ward?' the judge asked wearily. 'Then not today, if you please. I've had enough. And we have a long list. We adjourn until this day fortnight.'

'Postponing the inevitable, old boy,' Enderby murmured to Eric as they left court.

Back in his Quayside office Eric threw down the papers on his desk and walked over to the window to stare across at the bustle on the waterfront. There was a frigate moored on the Gateshead side: Tyneside was a favourite mooring for the matelots, and there were several gearing themselves up below his window, ogling some passing girls and waiting for the pubs to open. Eric felt vaguely unsettled, and had been so for several days, but he was unable to put his finger on the problem.

Quite clearly, the Broadlands affair lay at the centre of it all. When he should have been concentrating on his own practice, or listening to Anne as she talked of the progress of the Paulson affair, and her reluctant acceptance of the two million pound settlement her solicitor Davison, and Eric, had advised her to agree to, Eric yet found his thoughts drifting back to London. He thought of his conversation with Phil Cooper and dwelled on the malice that had glinted in Simon Wells's eyes when he had spoken of Pete Corsa. He thought of the dead woman he had never seen and wondered whether it had really been Corsa's rejection or Wells's using her that had pushed her to self-destruction. Or had it been her own weakness, and chosen life-style?

He would never know.

And then there was Eileen O'Hara.

The deadline for opening of the sealed bids in the leveraged buy-out was drawing near, and Eric would need to be present as O'Hara's adviser at the board meeting in London. Yet it was something else that kept drifting unbidden into his mind: Phil Cooper's question. Was Eric bedding her? The financial journalist had hinted at her sexual appetites; Eric himself had some evidence of the predatory sexuality she was capable of projecting. And though he should have dismissed such thoughts, they crowded back. It irritated him, annoyed him, but he could still remember the touch of her mouth and the line of her body, from that one occasion at her flat.

Money and sexual availability: Cooper suggested they were an aphrodisiacal combination.

True or not, it certainly made Eric's mind wander from business in hand. Consequently, he was relieved when the call finally came. It was like the resolution of a problem. The board meeting time and date had been confirmed: the sealed bids were in and would be considered the following Tuesday.

It was Eileen O'Hara who had placed the call, and he took it with mixed feelings.

'You'll be at the meeting, of course,' she stated, rather than asked.

Her voice had a husky quality that attracted him. 'I think I should be able to make it, without any problem.'

'I'm pleased. But there's something else turned up now. Another bid.'

'A third horse in the race?'

'Exactly. It's come from Paris. Manuel Ortega. He's acting for a European consortium. Do you know anything about him?'

'I don't. But maybe I can find out.'

It was time for another conversation with Phil Cooper.

There was a full turnout at the board on Tuesday. In addition to the directors Eric had met on his last appearance at Broadlands he was now introduced to two other men, seated beside Ted deSoutier. They were the managers who were involved in the bid with deSoutier: Neilson and Daly. They had smooth faces and worried eyes: there were echoes of their anxiety in their movements. Or maybe they were happier working in the company itself rather than facing members of the board.

Eileen O'Hara had arrived late at the offices so Eric had been unable to have a private conversation with her before the meeting. Now, as she opened the proceedings, she paid little attention to him, but headed straight for a confrontation with Ted deSoutier.

'You are aware that the main business of this meeting is to consider the sealed bids regarding the purchase proposals for Broadlands?'

'Of course.'

'I would have thought, therefore, that you, and Mr Neilson and Mr Daly, should have realized your presence here on this occasion was superfluous, if not embarrassing.'

'We all three hold seats on the board,' deSoutier replied stubbornly.

Eileen O'Hara was pale. 'But you have an interest in the proceedings.'

'Under the Articles of the company, Article 80 in fact, all we have to do is declare that interest, and then provided we take no part in the discussion, or vote on the matter before the board, we are entitled to remain.'

Subject to a formal resolution to the contrary, Eric thought. Ted deSoutier was right, of course, but Eric knew that this wasn't the point in issue. By their very presence, the three men were putting pressure on the board members: there would be a possible difficulty, with individuals reluctant to speak freely while de Soutier and the other managers were there. For a moment, Eric thought that O'Hara was going to issue an immediate challenge to the managing director. Then she cooled. She would be biding her time, Eric guessed. She looked at him, and there was fire in her glance. Then she turned to the company secretary.

'Mr Leslie,' she said sharply, 'would you now open the sealed bids, please.'

There was silence in the room. A few members of the press had gathered in the lobby of Broadlands, but had not been allowed up to the executive floor. O'Hara had promised a press release in due course. Now, the directors all waited as Leslie ripped open the large brown envelopes before him. There were three of them. He stared at the contents, shuffling them into order, wetting his lips with a nervous tongue, then he made a swift note of their contents and passed the sheaf of papers to his chairman.

Eileen O'Hara stared fixedly at the papers. Each bid was preceded with a summary sheet, with longer statements stapled behind, explaining in more detail the conditions and consequences of the bids. The room remained silent while she read. It was a good ten minutes, during which the room seemed almost electrically charged, before she raised her head. She spoke to the board, but she was looking directly at Ted deSoutier. There was nothing to be read in her dark features. Her voice was expressionless when she spoke, though her eyes seemed to hold a cold, dancing light.

'Gentlemen, I am able to report that Mr deSoutier has seen fit to raise his bid quite significantly. He now proposes an offer of forty million.'

There was a gasping sound from Andrew Strain, who straightened in his chair to stare at deSoutier. Neilson and Daly had paled, as though now they had heard the sum in someone else's voice they were having second thoughts about the size of the bid with which they were involved, but deSoutier's pugnacious jaw was set hard.

Hall Davies cleared his throat. 'That's thirty per cent above the original bid, for God's sake!'

'That's right,' Eileen O'Hara said quietly, her eyes still on deSoutier. 'It amounts to more than £9 per share.'

Strain shifted painfully in his seat and Tom Black leaned forward. His voice held a slight tremor. 'I take it we will not discuss the individual bids, but take all three first?'

'Of course,' Eileen O'Hara said calmly. 'There is a bid from Simon Wells. He too has now raised the level at which he's prepared to offer. In this instance, it seems Mr Wells is prepared to take his bid some twenty-five per cent higher . . .'

She paused, and deSoutier glared at her, unwilling to

believe what he thought he was hearing. Eric watched Eileen O'Hara, saw the malice in her eyes, and knew.

'... that is, twenty-five per cent higher than deSoutier's *original* bid,' she continued. 'Wells comes in at thirty-seven and a half million.'

Now they were all looking directly at deSoutier. His hands were shaking slightly: only a moment ago, as O'Hara had held him to his misconception, he had been terrified, desperate that he should have lost the bid. Now, as he heard the truth, and realized he had come in at a higher figure than Wells, his relief was patent, and mingled with a triumph that sent the blood rushing to his face.

'There is, however, a third bid,' Eileen O'Hara announced in a steely tone.

Ted deSoutier had overcome one crisis a moment ago, and now he was confident. He smiled arrogantly, and half turned to his colleagues Daly and Neilson. They were still pale, but excitement had now broken through and they were smiling.

'Let's have it,' Strain said harshly, angry suddenly at the cat and mouse game O'Hara seemed to be playing.

'The bid from Ortega, for the European consortium, is subject to certain conditions.'

'But the offer, in summary?' Tom Black asked.

'It's worth to Broadlands about forty-two million pounds.'

Her cold, flat tone silenced them. Neilson and Daly seemed stunned, frozen, their smiles turned into helpless grimaces, their disbelief struggling with their panic. Ted deSoutier's hands were suddenly still. He was glaring at O'Hara, fully aware now how she had played with him, a fish at the end of a financial line. There was a long, tense silence. Then deSoutier gathered himself. 'You bitch!' he grated.

She smiled thinly. 'I think you said yourself, it was not in order for you to speak on this issue. However, I'll disregard your ... comment. The board members have heard the outline of the bids. We can now enter details. But what is clear is that we must regard, for the benefit of our shareholders, the Ortega bid as the front-running one. Particularly since it's clear that in his initial valuation of the company Mr deSoutier would seem to have been ... ah ... widely astray. True, he has recalculated, but ...'

She let her words die away. Tom Black's eyes had narrowed, and he glanced briefly at the angry deSoutier before turning back to O'Hara. 'You said, Madam Chairman, that there are certain conditions attached to the Ortega bid.'

'They're not important,' she replied airily, enjoying deSoutier's fury. 'They relate to certain advantages the consortium expect to gain by way of tax write-offs. I think that when we look at the nature of the bid, this board will have no alternative but to accept the offer. Which will mean that the management buy-out proposed by Mr deSoutier is not acceptable, and the managers will need in due course to negotiate with Mr Ortega. I don't wish to pre-empt discussion, but at this stage we ought—'

Eric was staring at her. She caught his glance, and it gave her pause. She leaned forward. 'Mr Ward, you have no status at this board, other than as my adviser. But you wish to say something?'

'If the board will allow me.'

Andrew Strain raised an eyebrow; O'Hara looked at Hall Davies and Tom Black but neither made any demur. 'All right,' she said, 'what is it you want to say?'

'I would not advise a hasty acceptance of the Ortega bid.'

Ted deSoutier made a light hissing sound through his teeth. He leaned back in his chair, and thrust a nervous hand through his thick mane of dark hair. His eyes were as quick as ever, darting glances around the room, but they kept coming back now to Eric. Much of the arrogance had gone from his mouth, but there was a coiled tension in him that was communicated to all around the boardroom table.

Eileen O'Hara raised her voice a trifle, reluctance almost dragging the words back. 'Why are you suggesting caution?'

'You advised me that a bid was coming in from the Euopean consortium. I decided I should do some checking. The information I have managed to obtain is that the basis for the bid is suspect.'

'Suspect?' Andrew Strain almost exploded. 'What the hell is *that* supposed to mean?'

Eric glanced towards Eileen O'Hara, who hesitated, then nodded.

'We're all aware of the way things have been happening in the UK over the last four years,' Eric explained. 'Takeover activity has been hectic; UK companies have been raiding American assets, and more recently the corporations have turned their sights upon Europe. But in one sense the situation demonstrates how the market is a worldwide one: while corporate Britain attacked the United States, the Americans were actually targeting Europe.'

'All right, we all know the Americans put thirty-seven billion dollars into Europe last year,' Andrew Strain said cuttingly. 'So get to the point.'

'The merchant banks have been building up stakes in Europe,' Eric continued.' The main action has come from West Germany and France, then Italy and Spain. They missed out on the British spending spree in the States; they're determined not to lose out in Europe where it's the American investment banks that are grabbing most of the fees. And the fact is, now, that American investment houses have financial muscle in Paris—built up through Eurobond issues and American equity sales.'

Hall Davies frowned thoughtfully. 'What's this got to do with the Ortega bid?'

'Ortega is backed by a European consortium. But if you take a look at the consortium boardroom, my information is that the muscle there is American.'

Andrew Strain snickered unpleasantly. 'Come now, Ward, are you that chauvinistic that you advise against the bid because it might be American inspired?'

Eric shook his head. 'No. It's not that. I advise caution, for the simple reason that inquiries reveal the financial base for the European consortium is possibly not sound.'

'Are you saying Ortega couldn't finance the purchase?' It was deSoutier, unable any longer to restrain himself, aware suddenly that his hopes of success were alive again, with his bid looking more attractive against Eric's comments. O'Hara began to say something, angry at his intervention, but then thought better of it.

'I'm not saying Ortega couldn't finance the deal,' Eric said slowly. 'I counsel caution, and advise further investigation. In the States.'

'Why?' Tom Black asked.

'The information I have is that the financing is based upon certain US tax premises; advantages are assumed which may well be withdrawn. There is impending legislation in the States to close the loophole being used. If it is closed, it could become retroactive in effect; it could invalidate a deal struck with Broadlands; it could make it impossible for the Ortega group to go through with the implementation proposals. My advice is that an American tax lawyer should be consulted before anything further is contemplated with the Ortega bid.'

'Bloody hell,' deSoutier said, almost to himself. Some of the arrogance had come back to his mouth as he looked at Eileen O'Hara. He folded his arms, relaxing, and smiled, drumming his fingers against his biceps.

She was furious. A frown had gathered on her brow, and her mouth was stiff. She was staring at Eric, but she had heard deSoutier, and she was aware that the game she had played earlier was now reversed, the challenge thrown back upon her. She was struggling to master the anger she felt against her own adviser, and at the same time come to terms with the only realistic attitude to adopt towards the comments Eric had made.

'Mr Ward,' she said at last, in an icy tone. 'This information is . . . reliable?'

Eric paused, thinking of his conversations over the last few days with Phil Cooper. 'I have no reason to doubt it,' he said quietly.

She leaned back in her chair, glaring at the papers in front of her as though she wished she had never seen them. The silence grew in the room, heavy and overbearing. Eric waited. It was Ted deSoutier himself who broke the silence, foolishly and arrogantly, confident that he had won. 'Well, O'Hara, there's only one way forward, I guess.'

It stung her. She straightened. She paused for just a moment, eyes blazing at him, angry at his further interruption, and then she said, 'I think you're right. I intend to make a proposal from the chair. Such a proposal needs no seconder. It is simple. I propose that we extend the deadline for bids for Broadlands by another three days.'

'You can't do that!' deSoutier almost yelled.

'What the hell is there to stop me? The motion has been put to the board,' she snapped, 'and you're out of order in speaking to this matter.'

The chair crashed over as Ted deSoutier lurched to his feet, inflamed with anger. Neilson reached for his arm, tried to drag him back down, but the big man was beside himself with fury. He slammed his hands down on the table in front of him, leaning forward, almost spitting out the words. 'What the hell is it with you, O'Hara? Is it frustration? Is it because you've forgotten what it's like to have a real man in your bed? Or is it that you remember it only too well? Try to stick to the realities, for God's sake! This is *business* we're talking about, and the future of this company! We're not playing games. We're talking real money, and people's business lives and futures, and all you seem to want to do is to level old scores, get back at me in any way you can, and ignore what's best for the company! Your old man made a bad mistake when he left you in control of Broadlands; like any woman you don't think with your head; your brains seem to lie between your legs and the only worthwhile decisions you make are in bed! But I'm not taking this nonsense any longer—the board has to see that it's being subjected to the whims of a slut who—'

It was O'Hara's turn to rise. She opened her mouth to snarl back at the managing director of Broadlands, but it was Tom Black who got in first.

'*Eileen!*'

Both protagonists stopped, stared at him in surprise. He was cool; in control of himself. He glanced around the boardroom table to the controlling shareholders and directors of Broadlands. 'Mr deSoutier is out of order. I propose formally that he, and Mr Neilson and Mr Daly, be now asked to withdraw while the board discusses issues in which the three named have a declared interest.'

Hall Davies immediately grunted an assent. Andrew Strain followed quickly. Eileen O'Hara sat down and looked at deSoutier.

She paused, breathing hard. 'So that's agreed. You can go now,' she said at last, tight-lipped but in control of herself.

'All right,' deSoutier nodded. 'But remember—there's a price of £9 per share on the table!'

Tom Black was smiling slightly as the three managers left the room. In the silence that followed their departure Eric gained the impression that the deputy chairman of Broadlands was the only person in the room who seemed pleased at the turn of events.

2

Eileen O'Hara strode into the sitting-room of her flat, kicked off her shoes and almost threw herself into the deep armchair beside the window. She put her head back and stared at the ceiling. 'God, I need a drink!'

Tom Black looked back over his shoulder at Eric, smiled slightly, and walked across to the drinks cabinet. He poured his chairman a gin and tonic, clearly familiar with her needs in a crisis situation such as this.

'Mr Ward?'

'I'll have a small whisky.'

O'Hara turned her head and stared at Eric sourly. 'I could be better pleased with you.'

Eric was aware of Tom Black's curious glance. He waited until the deputy chairman of Broadlands handed him his whisky, then he turned back to Eileen O'Hara. 'You retained me to act as your adviser. That's just what I was doing.'

'I didn't like what I heard,' she replied grumpily.

'Oh, come on, Eileen,' Tom Black protested. 'That's hardly fair! You might wish to play games with deSoutier, but if the Ortega bid is as suspect as Ward suggests you can hardly be critical of him for raising the matter. It might be more important to you to score off deSoutier, but the board certainly—'

'All right, all right,' Eileen O'Hara interrupted irritably. 'You're right, you're both right, and I know it, but that bastard deSoutier—'

'You were able to let off some steam, both of you,' Black suggested.

'But where does that leave you now?' Eric asked.

Eileen O'Hara inspected him over the rim of her glass; her glance was ill-tempered, but calculating. 'You're my adviser. You tell me.'

Eric shrugged diffidently. 'I'm not sure. It depends upon whether you can take the board with you. Simon Wells has put in a bid which is lower than deSoutier's; if you discount Ortega's bid, and I believe you should, I would have thought you'd have difficulty in persuading the board they should not recommend deSoutier to the shareholders.'

'They've already supported me, in the extension of the bid deadline.'

'Reluctantly,' Tom Black reminded her softly.

'You voted with me,' she said to him. Her voice was scarred with undertones of anger and she glared at him, directly and challengingly.

Tom Black held up a placatory hand. 'Don't get me wrong, Eileen. I gave you my support, but I'm not at all happy about the way things are going. It may make sound business sense to throw open the bids again, and allow Wells to come back in with a counter-offer, but where does it end? And there's an ethical question here: if we give a deadline we should stick to it. I just don't understand your reasoning. I understand you have reason to dislike deSoutier, but this is business, and I would like to feel you have good reason for your behaviour today.'

'My arguments were presented to the board.'

'That you distrust him? Not good enough, Eileen. He's been doing well as managing director—why should we assume he can't turn the company around after a management buy-out?'

'You voted with me!'

Tom Black stared at her soberly. 'As a friend, Eileen. My head . . . well, let's just say I'd like to hear from you, now, whether you've any reason for pushing so hard against deSoutier at this stage in the game. Earlier on, in spite of your personal feelings about him, you'd have been prepared to go along with a management buy-out, for the good of the company and the shareholders.'

'Things have changed.'

'How?'

Eileen O'Hara glared at Tom Black, as though she was unwilling to be cross-examined by her deputy chairman. She hesitated, glanced at Eric as though for support and saw none. 'I don't trust him.'

'Not good enough, Eileen.'

'Damn it! All right, do you want me to spell it out? Look at the facts before us. Ted deSoutier has done well, you say, he's turned the company around, but now says the performance remains sluggish and the only way forward is his way, a management buy-out. OK, we agree, we ask him if we can see the colour of his money. So he makes a bid.'

'So?'

'So how come things change so radically once Simon Wells comes on the scene? Our friend deSoutier packages a proposal with the backing of the Melling Investment Bank —but as soon as a warship appears on the horizon, suddenly he and Pete Corsa are prepared to raise their bid by thirty per cent! For God's sake, what does that tell you about the man?'

'I'm not certain what you're implying,' Tom Black replied carefully.

'I'm not implying anything,' Eileen O'Hara said furiously, 'I'm stating a fact! The management group tried to pull the wool over our eyes: they know the business more intimately than we do—they're the managers—and they know its prospects. They came in with a cheap bid because they thought they could panic the board into a sale, after which they'd be making a hell of a lot of money for themselves and we'd be left nursing wounds. Just look at it! If deSoutier had put a fair price on the company to begin with, how come he's prepared to negotiate now at thirty per cent higher? The man's a crook!'

Tom Black hesitated. He glanced at Eric, sitting impassively, holding his untouched whisky. 'I think that's going over the top somewhat, Eileen. Ted deSoutier is a businessman—maybe there was an understating of the real value—'

'Understating! Hell's flames, Tom, thirty per cent! And have you seen what's been happening in the stock market these last few weeks? The public aren't fools: there's been a low trading position since Christmas, but then in the New

Year we saw a gentle rise in the value of the company. That's been going on steadily, even though there was no real explanation for a surge in confidence. But now, with this wrangling going on, the price is going through the roof —artificially. That won't do us any good in the long run, because the damn thing will crash again. But if deSoutier had put in a decent, acceptable bid in the first place, we'd have settled this and things would have been on an even keel.'

'Are you sure it would have been settled?' Tom Black asked quietly. 'Or would you have opposed the bid in any case?'

For personal reasons. He did not use the words, but they hung there in the air between them, unspoken, but real. Eileen O'Hara raised her chin defiantly: her eyes still held traces of anger, but her tone was cold. 'Maybe I would have. Perhaps you're right. But I still think my course is the correct one—let's reopen the bidding and see what happens.'

'The board doesn't like Wells's reputation.'

'And I don't like deSoutier.'

'You've talked of the man as though he's a crook, but some of the board would just say he's a shrewd businessman, trying to get the best deal for himself.' Tom Black shook his head thoughtfully. 'You're in trouble, Eileen. You'll have to come up with something stronger than this argument.'

'Something like breach of contract?'

Tom Black was still. He stared at his glass, frowning. Then he raised his head. 'Ted deSoutier's broken his contract of employment with us?'

'I suspect he's been feathering his own nest at our expense.'

'How?'

She was silent for several moments. 'I've . . . heard things.'

'Gossip?' Tom Black glanced at Eric as though seeking assistance, then turned back to O'Hara. 'You've got proof of shady dealings?'

'Not exactly.'

'Rumours, then. Can you bring any facts to the board.'

She pulled a grim face and Tom Black spread his hands despairingly. 'Come on, Eileen, it won't do. If you've got something on deSoutier, if you know of a breach of contract, then the board needs to know about it. But if all you're doing is making wild accusations just to back your case . . .' He paused, and there was a sudden tension in his frame as though he was deliberately taking a dangerous line of argument. 'Ted deSoutier threw you over, Eileen; I know that, and so does the board. But you should never have started the thing—and if you've got your pride hurt, that's your problem. It's another matter, trying to get back at him by suggesting he's corrupt.'

The room was suddenly cold. Eric was surprised by the personal nature of the comments from a man who seemed normally very much in control of himself. It was almost as though Tom Black had suddenly decided to upset Eileen O'Hara, deliberately. Eric frowned, watched Eileen O'Hara for her response. What he saw in her face caused a reaction in his own veins. It disturbed him. He now knew for certain she had had an affair with Ted deSoutier. He also knew that the thought left an ache in his chest.

'All right, Tom. Let's leave it there,' she said icily. 'I've heard deSoutier needs looking at. Take my word for it. But if you suggest I have personal reasons for a vendetta, what about your own?'

'I have no reason for a vendetta, Eileen,' he said quietly.

'But you've made your own mistakes too, haven't you?' she replied spitefully.

Tom Black stared at her for several moments. Then he finished his drink. He took a deep breath, and looked at

Eric. 'I'd better be on my way. The Ortega advice . . . the board's grateful, Ward, even if the chairman wasn't. I'll see myself out . . .'

The door closed quietly behind him and the room was filled with silence.

Eileen O'Hara rose and walked across to the cabinet to pour herself another stiff gin and tonic. There was a certain surliness in her dark face and her mouth was downturned with dissatisfaction, as though she felt she had said too much and handled the situation badly. She turned her back on Eric and stood staring out of the window. He had still not touched the whisky that Tom Black had poured for him. He set the glass down. 'I think it's time I went too.'

'No,' she said abruptly. 'Not yet.' She swung away from the window, and looked at him. 'Do you find me attractive?' When he hesitated she gave a short laugh. 'That's a stupid question. I know you do. I could tell, at the Mansion House, and again here, the last time you came to this flat. But you can never forget you're married to a poor little rich girl, can you?'

Eric felt angry. He rose from his seat. 'As I said—'

'You're not the controlled animal you pretend to be, I know that, my friend. And maybe you didn't like what you heard a few minutes ago . . . On the other hand, you're sharp, and maybe you already detected undercurrents in the board meeting, between me and deSoutier.' She laughed shortly. 'Oh, the hell with it! Of course we had an affair. He's an attractive man, and for a while . . . But he didn't throw me over.'

She paused, broodingly, her heavy eyebrows knitted in thought and memories she found disturbing. 'This isn't my business,' Eric said.

'Don't be so sure,' she snapped. 'Tom Black's only half right. Yes, I'd like to stick a knife into that bastard deSoutier.

He left me feeling . . . used, and I'm too big a girl ever to have that happen to me. But he managed it. I resent that.'

'I really don't think—'

'But put Tom's attitudes into context too. He's wanted me. He tried, once, and I laughed at him. You see, Tom thinks of himself as a bit of a ladies' man, but I know him. He has a ruthless, cold streak. Much like deSoutier, in fact. But his methods are different. Tom plays percentages; he'll always support me while I'm in the driving seat. Now, he's not so sure—but he's hedging his bets. He'll stay with me, if he's convinced he'll end up on the winning side. He thought by making a pass at me, he'd get an inside track in Broadlands. I don't react that way. So I told him to shove off. He'll never forget that.' She grinned, maliciously. 'And I'll never let him forget it.'

She walked slowly across the room until she was standing close to Eric. Her eyes were heavy-lidded. 'Some men arouse very positive reactions in me.'

'You mean men like Ted deSoutier?'

She smiled, but there was a wolfishness in her smile that removed any trace of humour. 'I like you, Eric. You're stiff; a bit withdrawn; you insist on being your own man. Stubborn as hell, I'd guess. But straight.'

'I used to be a policeman.'

'But now you're a lawyer. I've never regarded either as being particularly trustworthy. Anyway, no matter. You think my dislike of deSoutier is behind my arguments at the board.'

'Tom Black thinks so.'

'And he thinks all I've got is a bit of empty gossip. It's not so.'

'Gossip about deSoutier?' Eric paused, thinking. 'Do you really have any incriminating information about him?'

She pulled a face, twisting her mouth unpleasantly. 'I . . . I got an anonymous phone call. It suggested deSoutier isn't as clean as he might be. The voice was a woman's.

She'd clearly been drinking, and at one point she started to cry. But what she said was clear enough. Ted deSoutier's got some sort of fiddle going. And that's why I don't trust him—or his bloody bid!'

'A hysterical, crying woman,' Eric said quietly. 'Accusations over the phone anonymously? And about a man who you yourself admit is attractive? Are we talking about another discarded mistress?'

She didn't like it. Her mouth jerked, and for a moment he thought she was going to hit him. Then she managed a smile, cynical at the edges. 'Well, well. The shields are coming down a bit, Mister Ward. No, while I wouldn't put it past deSoutier—he's done enough playing around, of the kind Andrew Strain professes he'd like to do—but this woman, well, I'm not so sure . . . From what I know of her—'

'You know who phoned you?' Eric asked in surprise.

'Oh yes,' Eileen O'Hara replied. 'The anger, and the tears, and the self-pity, they all rolled up to make it a bit difficult . . . but I recognized the voice all right. I didn't need her to tell me who she was.'

'And the information she gave?'

'It was . . . vague. She was really just crying into her vodka. That's what she drinks. When she rang me she was sort of having a go against the Fates, bemoaning her lot, that sort of thing. But the gist of what she said is enough to make me want to hear more.' She leaned back, away from Eric, looking at him lazily, appraisingly. 'And I think maybe you should be the guy to tease the truth out of her.'

'I'm not sure—'

'Oh, come on, it's time you lived in the wider world. And after all, you've admitted to feeling a little surge for me, haven't you? Admitted to yourself, at least . . . Well, let's see if we can expose that weakness a bit more. This woman, maybe she's more your type. So go around to see her, Eric. Do it for me. Act like my big, brave adviser, and find out for me the truth about Ted deSoutier. It'll take courage. Not every husky young man wants to take on the challenge of a nubile, grieving widow!'

'What the hell are you talking about?'

'Haven't I made it clear, darling? I would like you to call on my informant, tease out of her the information she wouldn't give me over the phone. She lives in a flat, near Regent's Park. I can give you the address. Go there.'

'She—'

'She's called Cynthia. I don't think there's really been much grief about her widowhood. I'm sure she'd welcome your call.' Eileen O'Hara finished her drink and smiled. 'Cynthia . . . Cynthia Wishart. She'll have been missing her husband, ever since he got knifed by that mugger some months ago. So give her a call. But don't stay too long, Eric. I mean, all we want is some . . . information, isn't it?'

3

He could have refused. He still could refuse. Yet as Eric made his way towards Regent's Park, angry though he was with himself, he was also curious. He resented the way in which Eileen O'Hara seemed capable of reading him, teasing out inclinations he still denied in himself. But he was also curious about Cynthia Wishart. Her husband had been company secretary at Broadlands, and as such would have had an intimate knowledge of company affairs. As its compliance officer he would have been involved in all contractual relationships established by the company, so the importance of a phone call from his widow, suggesting there were matters to investigate in Broadlands, was obvious; it should not be taken lightly.

There was another side to it, of course. Cynthia Wishart's husband had been murdered in a casual attack near his home. She might well be lonely, in spite of what Eileen O'Hara had hinted at; she could possibly hold some resentment towards the company that had employed her husband; there was the chance that the tearful, inebriated call had been linked to some need to draw attention to herself, to feel wanted again now that she had retired into obscurity after her husband's death. These questions in Eric's mind drew him to Regent's Park: he would be taking the morning plane back to Newcastle so an early evening meeting with Cynthia Wishart was not too inconvenient for him.

He took a cab to Prince Albert Road and then walked towards Primrose Hill. The block of flats was modern, eight-storey, with balconies at the front overlooking the Park. A short flight of steps led to a security door: Eric checked the list of occupants and pressed the buzzer marked against Wishart. There was a brief delay and then, to his surprise, the disembodied voice invited him in, without checking his identity. The security door swung open to his touch, he entered the short hallway and took the lift to the fourth floor.

Cynthia Wishart lived in No. 35.

Eric rang the bell. He thought he heard a scurrying sound from inside the flat, as though someone was hurrying to the door. There was a spyhole at the level of his eye but the speed with which the door was opened suggested to him that Cynthia Wishart was not security conscious, because she opened to him without checking the spyhole.

She stood in the open doorway, smiling at him.

She was perhaps five feet three inches in height and doll-like in features. She had fluffy blonde hair, carefully disarranged. Her eyes were wide-spaced and china blue, her mouth generous, her figure noticeable. She would have been extremely nubile, as Eileen O'Hara had put it, when she was young: now, in her late thirties, she had begun to put on weight, giving a heaviness to her bosom and her hips that she would have been conscious of and concerned to remedy, or conceal. It could have accounted for the loose, flowing silk robe she wore, pale in colour, with a green dragon embroidered diagonally from left breast to right hip. It was the kind of casual attire she might use to relax in; on the other hand, it seemed hardly appropriate as clothing in which to entertain a stranger.

The smile was fading. She looked at Eric with a puzzled glaze in her eyes; her glance slipped briefly past him to the corridor beyond, as though she was checking that he had come alone, and then when she looked at him again there was a hint of alarm at the edges of her mouth.

'Mrs Wishart?'

'That's right.'

'My name is Eric Ward.'

A pink tongue touched nervous lips. Her left hand strayed to her throat and again she looked past him. 'What do you want?'

'I'd like to talk to you. I'm from Broadlands. Eileen O'Hara asked me to call to see you. I . . . I guess I should have rung, but I'm returning to Newcastle tomorrow so I took a chance . . .'

'Ward. I've never heard that name at Broadlands.' She frowned, looking him up and down. 'I'm not sure . . . do you have any identification?'

Eric took out his wallet. The only identification he had there was a Martin and Channing card, identifying him as a director. 'I'm sorry,' he said. 'This is my card . . . but I assure you, I'm here because of your phone call to Miss O'Hara.'

'Phone call?' For a moment she stared at him almost uncomprehendingly, and then a sudden alarm flooded into her eyes. She glanced past him to the corridor once more, then put a hand on his arm. 'You'd better come in.'

He stepped into the cramped hallway and she closed the door behind him. She walked ahead of him into the sitting-room. It was dominated by a huge, incongruous, highly decorated Indian urn, and the walls were hung with hunting prints. The room was a confusion of styles, as though in choosing furniture and decoration two minds had been at work, both uncertain, and neither agreeing with the other. There was a bottle of vodka on the coffee table, with a half empty glass beside it. Cynthia Wishart picked up the glass and drank from it, nervously and quickly, as if she needed it to face Eric. She turned, setting down the glass. 'Ward, you said.'

'That's right. I'm acting as an adviser to Eileen O'Hara at Broadlands and she asked me to call and talk over with you the remarks you made on the phone to her . . .'

Cynthia Wishart barely seemed to be listening. She stared at Eric's card, then she glanced at her watch. She sat down abruptly, leaving him standing. 'It was a mistake,' she half-whispered.

'I'm sorry?'

'The phone call. It was a mistake.'

Eric hesitated. 'Miss O'Hara suggested you were concerned about shady dealings in Broadlands—'

'No. A mistake. You've got to understand . . .' Her voice was shaky, as though her nervousness was increasing. 'I've not been well.'

'You mean your call to Miss O'Hara was . . . meaningless?'

'Yes. That's right. That's what I mean.' Cynthia Wishart glanced at the vodka bottle as though she needed its strength. 'You . . . you won't understand. What it's like, I mean. My husband . . . he was killed.' Her eyes were suddenly flooded with tears, but Eric was left with the feeling they were occasioned by self-pity as she hurried on. 'He was killed, and I was alone here . . . and there was no one to help any more. I was never involved with Broadlands, except socially sometimes, and my husband . . . Fred . . . he was a withdrawn man . . . older than me, we never went out, I had no friends and when he didn't come home that night . . . I was left with nothing, you understand, nothing!'

Except a good pension from Broadlands, and this flat at

least, Eric thought. There were no signs of poverty in the room. Perhaps the poverty lay in her own soul.

She fell silent, head lowered, staring at the carpet. Yet there was a watchfulness about her, an odd tension that made Eric feel she was waiting for something to happen, something unwelcome that could bring a crisis into her life.

'So the phone call—'

'It was . . . I just wanted to talk. I was . . . lonely. I wanted to talk, make someone feel I was important. It . . . it was a sort of cry for help.'

They didn't seem to be her words; it was as though she was reading from a script. She looked up at him, her eyes wide and slightly scared. 'I think you'd better go now. There's nothing for you here.'

He was inclined to agree.

When he stepped out into the street he looked back, up towards the fourth floor. A curtain twitched and quivered, but he could not be certain it was at Cynthia Wishart's flat.

Eric dined at his club and then phoned Eileen O'Hara. There was no answer from her flat; on an impulse he phoned the offices at Broadlands but the duty desk informed him she had not been in that evening. He went up to his room; there was a small balcony on which he stood, looking out over the Thames to the bright skyline of the South Bank. He felt unsettled.

The interview with Cynthia Wishart had been brief, and unsatisfactory. Something about it disturbed him, but he could not put his finger on the problem. There had been something wrong, unreal about her reception of him, and her attitude—nervous, uncertain, almost as though she were acting out some part—had left him confused.

And then there were the events of the day itself—the meeting at Broadlands, the outburst from deSoutier and the vindictiveness O'Hara clearly felt towards her former lover.

He tasted the words in his mouth. Former lover.

She provoked him in a way he did not understand. He admitted to himself that she was desirable, but he knew also it was a moth and candle situation that was dangerous—and unrewarding—for him. And though he found her desirable, he did not like her. Yet he was drawn.

As Tom Black had been, once.

Again, now, it seemed there was more calculation than friendship in Black's support of her at the board. The interlinking relationships at Broadlands ran more deeply than Eric had realized; they were more complex than was immediately apparent and consequently events were likely to be less predictable.

Here be dragons.

Eric was beginning to hope that the whole business would soon be over. He had promised, and contracted, to act as Eileen O'Hara's adviser. He would be glad to see the end of the contract.

Even as he thought so, something stirred inside him at the realization he would then have no further reason to see Eileen O'Hara.

He rang Anne in the morning, before he took the flight back north. He explained he needed to spend a day or so in the Quayside office.

'I'll see you Friday?' she asked.

'Early. I have a court appearance in the morning, but I should be able to get away at lunch-time.'

'That's good.' She sounded pleased. 'And how is business in London?'

'Nasty.' Eric hesitated. 'Anne, to be honest, I'll be glad to see the end of it.'

She was silent for a moment. 'OK. Let's hope it'll be soon. As for me . . . I've taken your advice, Eric. We've settled over the Paulson claim. We'll take the two million and run. Check it up to experience.'

'I think that's wise.'
'Hurry home.'
'Early Friday.'
He was back in Newcastle before lunch.

The next few days were hectic. There was a backlog of work in the office, and two formal dinners to attend in the spring business and professional round. Two new marine cases came in, one of them likely to take up a good deal of his time, and there was the Garrity case to prepare for. Oddly enough, Eileen O'Hara made no attempt to contact him; he tried to ring her once but again could not reach her. He left a message, so he could report to her on his interview with Cynthia Wishart but she did not return his call.

The newspapers gave wide coverage to the management buy-out position at Broadlands, but much of the reporting was conjectural. Eric checked Phil Cooper's column: the journalist had got it more or less right, and was of the view that deSoutier could well win through finally, because of his track record in the company, against the background of Simon Wells's reputation. But Cooper was not to know of the animosity lying between deSoutier and O'Hara—even though he was tuned in to City gossip generally.

On Friday morning Eric met Donald Enderby outside the courtroom. The solicitor was in good humour, clearly of the opinion that the case against Eric's client Garrity would quickly be dispensed with. The judge had been displeased that Eric even wanted to raise anything other than a paper defence, and Enderby expected the matter to be resolved quickly.

The judge was of the same opinion. Garrity was not in court when Eric rose to his feet. He had marked the relevant pages in the Law report on the table in front of him.

'If I may be allowed to recap,' Eric said, 'the facts are clear and not in dispute. My clients employ Mr Garrity. There is strong evidence to suggest that this gentleman, addicted to horse-racing as he is, may well have placed bets over the phone lines of offices he was employed—by my clients—to clean.'

'And the contract, Mr Ward, don't forget the contract,' the judge rumbled, bored.

'The contract is clear. It states the firm is strictly liable for the acts of employees while they are on the premises of clients.'

'And that,' the judge said, 'is that.'

'Not quite so,' Eric suggested.

'Oh, come on, Mr Ward,' the judge responded irritably, while Enderby wriggled in delight. 'The situation is quite clear. The contract is positive—and in such a case the employers, the cleaning firm, your clients, must be regarded as vicariously liable for Mr Garrity's wrongdoing. Really, I have to say you are wasting our time. Even if there were no such clause in the contract, the weight of precedent is such that I would be forced to find there was an implied term in such an agreement, in order to give the contract business efficacy. Your clients have to accept responsibility for Garrity's actions on the premises!'

'With respect,' Eric said quietly, 'there can be no vicarious liability for those acts of Mr Garrity which are wholly outside the scope of his employment. He was employed to clean the offices; he was *not* employed to make phone calls. He was therefore indulging, as the precedents say, in a "frolic of his own". For this "frolic" my clients cannot be held responsible.'

Enderby shuffled, and stood up. He cleared his throat nervously. 'If I may intervene . . . while the general rule is certainly that which Mr Ward outlines, the fact is we must imply the relevant term, because the only reason Garrity was able to make the phone calls was that the defendants put him in those offices.'

'To *clean*,' Eric insisted.

'Yes, but he was thereby given the opportunity to make

the calls. And that must be the responsibility of the defendants. So vicarious liability must follow.'

The judge glowered, and turned to Eric. 'Well?'

Eric shrugged. 'An interesting argument . . . but unsoundly based. It is not enough merely to provide opportunity: in order to incur vicarious liability for acts outside the scope of employment it must be shown that there is a nexus between the circumstances of the employment and the act . . . not just opportunity.'

The judge's frown deepened. 'You have authority for that statement?'

'The case of Heasmans and Clarity of 1987.'

Enderby hissed through his teeth, involuntarily. The judge glanced in Enderby's direction and heaved a sigh. 'Give me the reference. But if Mr Ward is right . . .'

'And are you?' Enderby asked as they left the courtroom.

'Check it out for yourself,' Eric suggested. 'Youll find that though Mr Garrity may well have committed a criminal offence, his employers can't be held vicariously liable—even though they provided him with the opportunity—because the act was outside his employment and there is no connection between the act and the circumstances.'

'Your clients will be pleased,' Enderby grumbled, 'even if Garrity isn't. He'll have to face the music alone, now.'

'*If* proceedings are taken against him. Your clients may feel it's hardly worth while. Garrity will get sacked, and maybe a criminal charge will be brought—but oddly enough, I don't think he's particularly bothered.'

Nor was he.

Eric was back at his office, clearing his desk before he headed north for Sedleigh Hall, when reception rang to tell him Garrity wanted to see him. Eric refused at first, but when they told him Garrity was insistent, he agreed that they should allow the man up to his room.

'Garrity, it's been a long week and I'm going home. Make it short.'

In spite of his frayed cuffs and grey, unshaven cheeks, Garrity had a jaunty air. 'Sure, I wanted to thank you, Mr Ward, that's the size of it.'

'Your employers are off the hook, but you aren't,' Eric warned grumpily.

'Ah, that's not important. It's the principle of the thing, you know?' Garrity rolled his yellow-tinged eyes theatrically. 'I could get a bad reputation, Mr Ward, if other people were to be held responsible for my actions.'

'*Reputation?*' Eric looked at the shabby Irishman in amazement. 'I wouldn't have thought you had much reputation to lose. And the police—'

'Ah, sure, if they lay this on me, it'll only be a short while inside. That's no great tribulation. But who'd be after employing me again, if you hadn't got me employers off this time?'

Eric shook his head. 'Garrity, I think you live in a different world from the rest of mankind.'

Garrity grinned. 'It's me upbringing, sir.'

'OK, but I've got to go now and—'

'Just the one other thing, Mr Ward.' Garrity grinned widely. 'Me life is not spent entirely in a wasteful manner.'

'What's that supposed to mean?'

'A feller can hear a great deal at the racetrack—apart from the jockey's obscenities, that is.'

'Such as?'

'Such as your good lady's been involved somewhat of recent months in some business with a certain Mr Eddie Paulson.'

'How do you know that?' Eric asked suspiciously.

'Sure, it's common gossip. And there's more. The story is, a court action was avoided, as they say, by a judicious agreement to settle a large sum of money out of court.' Garrity scratched his unshaven cheeks with a dirty fingernail. 'Now am I right, Mr Ward?'

'You get around, Garrity.'

'And I see and hear things,' Garrity winked. 'Like last Saturday, at Newcastle. The bookies were walkin' around with wide smiles.'

'Don't they always?'

''Specially this time. A lot of money got thrown away on an outsider that remained just that. It never came in at all. A certain individual lost money. A hell of a lot of money.'

Eric stared at him. 'And who might this person be?'

'Why, to be sure,' Garrity grinned, 'your lady's business acquaintance, Mr Paulson. I just thought you'd like to know, Mr Ward, seein' as you'd helped me reputation. You scratch my back, as they say, and I'll scratch yours. But fact is, the gossip says that Eddie Paulson—he's *really* on his uppers now!'

After Garrity had gone Eric sat down, thinking. The information was interesting, but hardly important. Anne had settled the suit with Paulson on Eric's and Davison's advice. If Paulson then chose to celebrate by visiting the racetrack that was his business. If he lost money, that also was his business—provided he could afford it. If not ... the settlement with Monarch Estates could be in jeopardy. Eric frowned. He thought of ringing Anne, but decided it could wait: the information was nothing they could act upon immediately. He would be able to talk it over with Anne that evening.

He made his way down to reception.

'Any appointments fixed for Monday?'

'Just this one, Mr Ward. Mr Davison wants an hour with you.'

Anne's solicitor. Eric didn't like him, and couldn't imagine why the man would want to see him. Their business lives rarely crossed. He considered for a moment. It could be something to do with what Garrity had just told him. He nodded. 'Right. Book him in for ten o'clock. And now, I'm away.'

The door had opened behind him.

The man standing there had thick, springy hair that was greying at the temples. He had a straggly moustache that seemed to emphasize the discontent of his mouth, and his blotchy skin sagged over a fleshy jowl. Eric saw him standing there, stocky, powerful in his ill-fitting suit, and there was a sour taste in his mouth. He knew him; it meant trouble.

'Mr Ward. Just going out?'

'Detective Superintendent Mason,' Eric said carefully. 'I'm just heading home.'

'Ah,' Mason intoned. 'Sorry to detain you.'

He wasn't. 'What do you want?' Eric asked.

'A brief word. In private.'

'I'm going home.'

'It won't take long.'

'Can't it wait until Monday?'

Mason smiled unpleasantly. 'I don't think so. Hate to delay your weekend, of course. Nothing to do with me, though, really. I'm just doing a favour for the Met. It's their pigeon, after all.'

'What do you mean?'

'Well, it's a Met case, but they referred this matter up to me, since you're Newcastle based, like. To make some inquiries.'

'Inquiries?'

'That's right, canny lad. You were one of the last people, it seems, to see Mrs Cynthia Wishart.' As he saw the expression on Eric's face, malice scored the detective's mouth. 'But perhaps you hadn't heard she's been found dead?'

He sighed theatrically. 'Why aye, that's right. Dead.' He grinned, wolfishly. 'Dead and cold as mutton, it seems.'

CHAPTER 5

1

Colonel Sanderson-Gilbert was one of those people who was easily entertained as a dinner guest. All that was required was to sit down and listen to him. In fact, Eric concluded as Anne's dinner-party wore on, one didn't even need to listen: he seemed not to notice the glazed inattention of his fellow guests as he meandered on, dominating the conversation.

'Surely,' he was concluding a story that had seemed to run on interminably, 'you're not going to eat your steak alone! Those were her very words. And I replied, "Certainly not! I'm going to eat it with potatoes!"'

Sanderson-Gilbert roared with laughter and wiped his moustache with his table napkin. Eric was aware of someone standing just behind his shoulder. He turned.

'There's a phone call for you, Mr Ward.'

'I'll take it in the library.'

He caught Anne's glance. She raised her eyebrows; he shrugged, made his excuses and left the table. Sanderson-Gilbert hardly seemed to notice. 'So the waiter asked me how I found my steak. I told him I moved the peas and potatoes and *then* I found it! . . .'

Eric closed the library door gently behind him and drowned out the sound of forced laughter from the dining-room.

'Hello? Ward? What the hell is going on?'

Eric was tempted to say Sanderson-Gilbert was going on. Instead, he said, 'Hello, Leonard. A Saturday night call? Have you nothing better to do?'

'I certainly have, but when something of this magnitude arises I'm forced to break in upon the peace and quiet of your elegant Northumberland retreat! I presume you have an explanation for it all?'

'For what, Leonard?'

'Your involvement with this Wishart thing!'

'News travels fast.'

'But not enough of it!' Leonard Channing sounded cold but sharp; he was in control of himself but there was a dangerous note in his voice. 'I want to know what explanation you have to give for dragging Martin and Channing into your sordid affairs.'

'Careful, Leonard. It's very easy for me to hang up. And unless you choose your words with a little more care, I'm inclined to do so.'

'You can't bluff your way out of this one, Ward. I've no idea what your connection with Cynthia Wishart was; I've no interest in your social life. But when it intrudes upon the firm—'

'Now hold on—'

'You deny she knew you as a representative of Martin and Channing?'

'That wasn't the way of it.'

'So how was it that she had one of our cards with your name on it?' Leonard Channing paused sneeringly. 'Away from home, up there in Newcastle, maybe you think you can get entry to all sorts of places by using a Martin and Channing card, but I know the board will be less than pleased to hear I had a visit from the police asking about you—one of the directors on the board. They came and asked me what I knew about this woman Wishart, and then produced your card . . . Of course, I had to disclaim knowledge and refer them to you in Northumberland—'

And Detective-Superintendent Mason, Eric thought sourly.

'—but it seems to me this all ties in with your ill-advised

decision to act for that woman O'Hara. This Wishart person was the widow of the Broadlands company secretary, wasn't she? Now I really don't want to know the answer, because it seems to me Martin and Channing is already tied in with too many issues over Broadlands to want to know more.'

'You say ill-advised, Leonard, but it was you who introduced Eileen O'Hara to me—'

'So am I your keeper?' Leonard Channing gave a short barking laugh. 'An introduction is one thing; a retainer with her firm is another. As for this Wishart thing . . . look, Ward, I don't know how I'm going to cover this up with the board—'

Not that he'd even try, Eric thought; this was a chance to thrust in some needles, under the fingernails.

'—because as you're aware we're now seriously proposing to support the Corsa financial package in the leveraged buy-out of Broadlands shares. Martin and Channing can retain their distance, and their integrity, by using Corsa as the intermediary. But the latest story I have is that, in spite of having you as an adviser, the board has refused to accept deSoutier's bid, is calling for a new deadline—'

'*Has* called,' Eric interrupted.

'—and you must realize that is against the interests of Martin and Channing.'

'Leonard,' Eric said calmly, 'I advise Miss O'Hara, not the Broadlands board. And in that capacity I do not represent Martin and Channing. So their interests are irrelevant.'

'You are still a director of Martin and Channing. And therefore there's a conflict of interest.'

'I disagree. I entered the O'Hara contract before you started talking with Corsa.'

'A matter of timing does not remove the basic argument.' Channing's tone took on a certain silkiness. 'It's time you withdrew from the Broadlands contract. Or alternatively, from the board of Martin and Channing.'

And either way, Eric thought, I'd lose. Leonard Channing's game was obvious. If Eric withdrew from Broadlands, Leonard would make it clear to everyone in the City that Eric had dishonoured an agreement and let down a client; if he resigned from Martin and Channing there would be whispers of a different kind, scurrilous whispers he would be unable to control or refute. He smiled coldly. 'I intend doing neither, Leonard. If you want to go to the board with some concocted story of conflict of interest, fine. I'll argue my own corner.'

'And the Wishart thing? We won't be happy about being touched by sordid episodes from Regent's Park—'

Eric put down the phone. Leonard Channing would not have enjoyed being cut off. But Eric took little pleasure in the thought. Ever since Detective-Superintendent Mason had visited his office he had known there would be City repercussions.

He went back to the dining-room.

'. . . and she asked me if I knew what made the Tower of Pisa lean, and I said I didn't, because if I did I'd take some! . . .'

Sanderson-Gilbert was still uttering his inanities. Anne caught Eric's glance, and smiled supportively. She could guess from whom the call had come. 'I think it's time for coffee,' she suggested.

Later, they sat in the darkened sitting-room, just the two of them, with soft music playing in the background, Eric with a brandy, Anne with a gin and tonic. 'I had a feeling,' Anne said, 'that one of them was almost bound to say at the door, "I've had a wonderful evening . . ."'

'"But this wasn't it!"' Eric finished for her. He smiled. 'Sanderson-Gilbert really can be a bore. He's the kind of motorist who'll never run out of gas. Ah, to hell with it. I feel dog-tired.'

'That's because you've been growling all day.'

Eric grinned. 'Have I been that bad?'

'Worse.' Anne hesitated. 'You've been . . . preoccupied. Don't you think it's time you told me about it, in detail? All I know so far is that Mason visited you, questioned you about the death of this woman Wishart. And now this evening Leonard's rung you to twist the knife. Talk to me, Eric.'

It would help, he knew. He shrugged. 'Mason was at his most objectionable.'

'That can be something, I know!'

'He insisted I went up to my office—after he'd made an announcement in reception which would have caused tongues to wag.'

'Your staff are loyal, Eric,' Anne said softly.

'But human . . . Still, Mason began by pointing out they knew I'd been to see her at Regent's Park because they found my Martin and Channing card there. I had little enough to tell him, of course, and besides . . . I was confused.'

'How do you mean?'

'It's not easy to explain. You see, Anne, when I arrived at the Regent's Park flat and rang the bell she let me straight in through the security door. She didn't check on my identity. The same thing happened at the door to the flat itself. She didn't check me out. Only after she saw me standing there in the doorway did she ask for identification. All I had was the Martin and Channing card.'

'Then she let you in.'

Eric nodded. 'But she was preoccupied, edgy. And it was as though she was sort of listening for something, waiting.'

'For what?'

'I don't really know. I went there to find out why she rang Eileen O'Hara with some hints of corruption on deSoutier's part, but she denied there was anything to it. She'd just been seeking attention in her loneliness after her husband's death. And yet . . .'

'Yes?'

'I don't know. I got the feeling at the time . . . she was sort of playing a part, acting out some story.'

'I don't understand.'

Eric shook his head. 'Nor do I, exactly. But it was as though . . . well, as though she was waiting for someone to come, or something to happen.'

'Did you tell Mason this?' Anne asked.

Eric hesitated. 'Not until later.'

Mason had sat there in front of him. bull-necked, leaning forward to listen with his fingers loosely linked together, left hand in right, confident, arrogant and malicious. They had clashed often enough in the old days, because when they were on the Force together Eric had made no secret of his dislike of the man's violent methods of dealing with weak, petty criminals. Since he had taken to the legal profession Eric had found himself in direct contention with Mason in the police courts from time to time, and Mason had not enjoyed the experience. Now, any chance he could get to put pressure on Eric was a chance to savour.

'So when you left, she was sort of dressed in a robe with a dragon on it, was she?' he had asked.

'That's right.'

'Anything underneath?'

'I imagine so,' Eric had replied drily.

'Didn't check, hey?' Mason sneered insinuatingly. 'Funny that, though. I mean, the dragon robe. That wasn't what she had on when she died.'

'So?'

'It was a dressing-gown. And nothin' else.'

'You told me the theory is she died about two in the morning.'

'Preliminary. Hour or two earlier, maybe. When you say you were at your club. Still sticking to that?'

Eric controlled his tongue. 'That's right.'

'Funny, though, isn't it? I mean, going to bed, then

walking out into the corridor again. Scantily dressed, to say the least. And what did she want in the garage?'

'What garage?' Eric asked evenly.

'Oh, come on, didn't you know those flats had an underground garage? Four floors up, she was, and the garage in the basement. The Met tell me she was found in the stairwell. She'd gone out of her flat, along the corridor, down the steps, and then fallen. Drunk as a cat. Car keys beside her. Vomit on the stairs. Wearing a dressing-gown. Crazy, don't you say so, hey, bonny lad?'

When Eric remained silent Mason had sniggered. 'But then, it all happened after you'd gone. You'd been asking questions, is that it? About Broadlands? But she had nothing to say. So she drinks half a bottle of whisky on top of what she'd had before, staggers out into the corridor, ignores the lift and heads for her car. She's sick on the stairs, falls over the rail, breaks her neck in the stairwell. And you got no ideas about why?'

'None.'

'Maybe she was disappointed.'

'In what?'

'Your performance,' Mason leered.

'That's not funny.'

'Maybe that's what she thought. "Hey, that wasn't funny," she thought, walked out and broke her neck...' Mason twisted his mouth unpleasantly. 'Anyway, if you've nothing more to add to your story, perhaps we could take a formal statement. And I can ask you if you're prepared to take a test.'

Eric frowned. 'A test?'

'That's right. Didn't I tell you?' Mason's feigned surprise could not mask the malicious glee in his eyes. 'This merry widow of yours, this Cynthia Wishart, she'd been humping it before she died. The preliminary investigation disclosed she'd had it away. There were bruises on her thighs, traces of semen... Now a public-spirited citizen like you, I'm sure you won't mind helping us coppers in our inquiries.' Mason had given an evil chuckle. 'Just by letting us just check out whether there's a match—whether it was you who screwed Cynthia Wishart, a short while before she died.'

Anne was silent for a while. The music came to an end but neither of them rose to change the disc. The room was warm and dark and he was unable to see her face clearly, but her breathing was slow and regular. She could almost have been asleep. He knew she wasn't.

'So it was only *then* you told Mason you thought she'd been waiting for something when you arrived.'

'I don't think she'd been waiting for some*thing*. She was expecting some*one* at the flat. The bell rang, she opened the doors. She was surprised to see me. And then she remembered, and got defensive.'

'Remembered what?'

Eric sighed and shook his head. 'I don't know. Her script. Her story. I don't know. Anyway, there's one thing for sure —there's no way they can tie me to Cynthia Wishart by any tests.'

'I never believed there would be, Eric.'

For some reason, her quiet reassurance only brought the image of Eileen O'Hara to his mind. To dismiss it, he said, 'So what about Garrity's story, then?'

'Eddie Paulson at the races? I can't see how he can afford to spend anything! But I'll get on to Davison on Monday, see what he can find out.'

'Maybe I can find out for you. He's booked in to see me at ten.'

'Davison? What about?'

'Who knows?'

They were silent for a while, each deep in personal thoughts. Eric rose and replenished Anne's gin; he took another brandy himself. He was aware Anne was watching him, curiously: one glass of alcohol was the rule, normally. But things were hardly normal. He walked across to her and perched himself on the arm of her chair, slid one hand across her shoulders. She put her head back.

'I'm glad you're home.'

'But back to the Quayside on Monday.'

'And London?'

He was silent for a few moments, aware of the unbidden tension of her neck against his fingers. 'The board meets Monday evening. I've told Broadlands I can't make it. They're taking a decision on the two bids. They don't need me to make up their minds.'

'I think Eileen O'Hara needs you . . . Or wants you.'

'And *I* . . . want *you*,' he said and kissed her.

2

The drive down to Newcastle from Sedleigh Hall was pleasant. He set off at six-thirty and there was a frost in the fields, glistening under the sharp morning rays of the rising sun. At his back the line of hills was dark-shadowed, knife-rimmed; two early morning riders, young girls, raised their hands to him as he drove past their skittish mounts, and then shortly afterwards he was out on to the open road, moving quickly along the dual carriageway south to the city, with the long blue coastline to his left, shimmering under the glittering sun.

Traffic was building up on the North Road as he entered the city but he was early enough to miss the worst of it. To the south, he knew, the daily trek would be well advanced; there was evidence of it when he reached his office on the Quayside, for the Tyne Bridge was already jammed with cars, commuters from County Durham thrusting into the town.

Charles Davison arrived promptly at ten. Eric paid his fellow solicitor the courtesy of not keeping him waiting. Davison entered and shook hands, then sat down.

He had the rugged good looks of a male model, craggy yet with soft planes to his features, eyes too brown, jaw too regular, cleft in the chin too pronounced. He had long eyelashes that served to hide eyes that could be guileful. A slightly built man, he was sharp suited; a gold wrist chain gleamed on his left wrist and his shirt and socks were of matching colours. He was a successful solicitor, in spite of his reputation with his professional colleagues, and he moved in the best circles, picked up the best contracts. He was in his early forties, and he remained active: his figure demonstrated a reputed addiction to squash, and his tan suggested he spent as much time as possible out of doors.

'It's good of you to see me at such short notice, Ward,' he said, in a deep, agreeable voice. He glanced around him at the small office. 'Cosy.'

Eric smiled and Davison caught the smile. 'Sorry,' he added. 'That sounds patronizing.'

'The office suits me.'

'And your Quayside practice has a sound reputation. No fear or favour, I understand.'

'Is that why you're here?' Eric asked. 'Not to consult me, surely!'

'You seem surprised.' Davison fingered the cleft in his chin a little self-consciously. 'I can't imagine why. I mean, if a lawyer gets into trouble, he can hardly advise himself.'

Eric leaned back in his chair. He was intrigued. Davison had used the word 'trouble'. Up till now Davison had avoided trouble—sailed close to the wind, certainly, but kept clear of the rocks.

Davison frowned, as though he had read Eric's thoughts. 'Perhaps trouble is rather overstating the case.'

'So state it,' Eric said abruptly.

'It's the Eddie Paulson business,' Davison replied and watched Eric carefully.

The morning sun was still bright, and now it shone directly through Eric's office window, glittering on the silver paperknife on the edge of the desk. The room was silent; from the Quayside there came the hum of traffic, and from the offices below Eric's there was the faded murmur of voices in reception. 'Paulson,' Eric said at last. 'You're handling that settlement issue on behalf of Morcomb Estates.'

'Your wife, that's right.'

'Morcomb Estates,' Eric repeated carefully.

'As you will.'

'So what's the problem?'

Charles Davison inspected his cuff, flicked away an invisible speck and smiled thinly. 'I suppose the problem, in a nutshell, is simply that Eddie Paulson is not a gentleman.'

Eric almost laughed. The remark held a certain incongruity in Davison's mouth. 'I always thought a gentleman was someone who could show you his home movies, but doesn't.'

Davison was not amused; he bared his teeth. 'Funny. What I mean is, Paulson makes a bargain and then doesn't want to stick to it.'

'The settlement with Morcomb Estates?'

Davison hesitated. 'Well, not exactly. It's sort of . . . contingent upon that. But . . . no, the settlement is still on, contracted for. It's the collateral contract that Paulson's bitching about.'

'Collateral contract,' Eric repeated flatly. He stared at the solicitor facing him; he had the feeling from the tension that was beginning to show in the man's bearing that there was something amiss in the conversation. For a moment he thought he should draw the discussion to an immediate close, and have nothing further to do with Anne's solicitor. His curiosity got the better of him. 'Just what do you mean by the phrase—collateral contract?'

Davison shrugged uneasily, and avoided Eric's eyes. 'I don't know how you handle your business, Ward. As far as I'm concerned, I don't hold with the ridiculous arguments that are often raised by some lawyers. I'm a businessman, and I deal with businessmen. Professional rules are fine, but not if they inhibit legitimate business deals.'

'We're still talking about the settlement with Morcomb Estates.'

Davison nodded. 'When your wife briefed me, I realized it was not going to be an easy business. First of all, there was the sum of money involved—four million, for God's sake! Then there was Paulson. Eddie Paulson is not the easiest of men to work with: he's a braggart, a loudmouth, and he's slippery as a snake. There would have been a hell of a problem bringing him to court over that four million —it would have cost the earth. So I advised your wife to settle.'

'So did I.'

Somewhat startled, Davison looked up. 'Nice to know we're of a mind. Anyway, the fact is Paulson wasn't easy to pin down. And he was never really convinced that Morcomb Estates would settle. He felt he'd be better out of it by going bankrupt. He's done it before. I . . . I finally persuaded him that it would be in . . . in everyone's interests to enter the settlement. I got him to agree to a figure of two million. It was better than he'd hoped for. He was still reluctant. I finally gave him a virtual guarantee that I could swing it.'

'A guarantee?'

'Provided he paid my fee.'

Suddenly it was out in the open. Eric sensed it. He stared at Charles Davison; the man met his glance boldly enough, but he was paling. 'A fee,' Eric repeated.

'Payable in advance.'

'How much?' Eric asked harshly.

Davison hesitated. 'The sum, in question is . . . a hundred and fifty thousand pounds.'

In reception someone laughed; the sound echoed faintly up to them. 'That's a hell of a lot of money to—as you put it—swing a deal with Morcomb Estates,' Eric said coldly.

'Don't get stuffy with me, Ward. You know that settlement was in your wife's interests. You told me you yourself would have recommended it.'

'But I wouldn't have charged Morcomb Estates that kind of fee!'

'I didn't charge Morcomb Estates. I charged Eddie Paulson.'

'By suggesting you could swing something no one else could.'

'I did nothing illegal,' Davison insisted hotly. 'There's nothing wrong in both sides paying for my skills, as long as it's only one side I legally represent! Let's just call it a commission from him, for doing the deal between the two parties.'

'Commission,' Eric said softly. 'All right. So did he pay?'

Davison nodded. 'As I told you, it had to be up front—or I wouldn't use my best efforts towards a settlement.'

'He didn't know Morcomb Estates were already prepared to settle.'

'The fact was irrelevant. So he paid.'

'So what are you talking to me for?' Eric asked scornfully. 'You got what you wanted. You milked Eddie Paulson by conning him into paying for something it was in Morcomb's interests to do anyway. Where's your big problem?'

Davison cleared his throat uneasily. 'He wants his money back.'

'He *what*?' Eric grinned broadly. 'Now I really know what's bothering you!'

'Do you?' Charles Davison straightened in his seat. 'I don't intend returning the money, of course. If Eddie Paulson reaches a bargain with me I expect him to keep to it. The fact that he's strapped—'

'Unwise investment in the racetrack, I understand.'

'—that's *his* problem! He's instructed a solicitor to act for him. I got the details last week. Paulson's asking for a return of my commission—the hundred and fifty grand—together with an account of all profits earned by the sum.'

'Nice.'

'I want you to act for me. I want you to defend the claim.'

Eric almost laughed aloud in his face. He had made no secret of his dislike for Davison and his methods; he had advised Anne against retaining him. Yet now the man was asking him to defend an indefensible position. He leaned forward, about to tell Davison to go to hell, when Davison said, 'Of course, there is, otherwise, the problem of the settlement.'

'What do you mean?'

'Things get . . . tainted by association. You know, smoke and fire, that sort of thing.'

Eric stared at the solicitor for a few moments uncomprehendingly, then suddenly knew exactly what he meant. Davison was going to resist Paulson to the bitter end. And that could mean involving other people in the 'commission' arrangement. Davison was making it quite clear: if Eric refused to defend him, it was Morcomb Estates—and Anne —who would be the loser. Davison would say that it was Anne who had asked him to do the commission deal—or that it was done with Morcomb Estates connivance.

'They say you have the reputation of being straight,' Davison remarked after a little while.

It was likely to be the only explanation Eric would get for Davison's insistence on using the Quayside firm. On the one hand, for Anne, guilt by association, on the other, for Davison, having a lawyer acting for him with a reputation for probity.

Or maybe it was just that he wanted to drag Eric Ward down with him into the gutter.

'If this conversation got out . . .' Eric said quietly.

'It can't. You won't say a word. The conversation is privileged.'

'You're not my client.'

'As good as. I'm consulting you over a legal problem. You try to expose what I've said, not only will I deny it but

I'll sue. And the Law Society will hear of your breach of faith.' Davison smiled thinly. 'You might not think much of me as a lawyer, Ward, but I've read the books.'

Eric stared at him angrily. The man was right. Communications between client and lawyer were privileged, and the privilege lay with the client: it was up to Davison to give permission to disclose the conversation, not Eric.

And the unspoken threat still lay in the background.

'I'll have to think about it,' Eric said.

'Fine. But don't take too long. And make the right decision.'

Eric did think about it, during the course of the afternoon. It lay constantly at the back of his mind, distracting him from other business in hand. The dilemma was clear: Davison wanted his reputation and ability in his resistance to Eddie Paulson's demands, and if he refused Anne would be dragged into the whole sordid, back-handed business. It seemed to Eric he had little choice, though the thought infuriated him.

Some of the anger was still with him when he received a call in the late afternoon from Eileen O'Hara; it must have been reflected in his response.

'What's the matter with you, Eric? You sound like a bear with a sore backside!'

'Just business. What can I do for you?'

'Crisp! OK, I won't inquire more,' she said snappishly, echoing his own mood. 'The fact is, the board meeting's just ended. I got my way, but it wasn't easy.'

'So the decision's been made? You've gone for Simon Wells?'

She laughed throatily. 'No, that would have been expecting too much from the board. We had a long and stormy meeting. You won't be surprised to hear I was certainly going for Wells but there was opposition. Andrew Strain is behaving oddly these days: he seems to be unable to make up his mind, or maybe he's playing some deep game. Hall Davies is with me, of course: he's been backing the Wells bid all along.'

'And Tom Black?' Eric asked.

'Tom seems to be swaying with the wind. It's almost as though he's agreeing with whoever spoke last. It means he's constantly shifting his ground.'

'Is that characteristic?'

She was silent for a few moments. There was a distant crackling on the line. 'Well, I wouldn't have said so. The normal pattern is that as vice chairman he's tended to support me. But he clearly has doubts about my judgement on this one. So I've not been able to read him: I thought at one stage he was going to go for deSoutier and Corsa—then suddenly he was speaking against it again.'

'But you got what you wanted.'

'More or less. I want to nail that bastard deSoutier's colours to the mast, so everyone can see. When I realized I'd have difficulty pushing through the Wells bid from a lower baseline than deSoutier's, I proposed one last try. An auction.'

'What?'

'An auction,' she repeated calmly. 'A final chance for both of them to make an acceptable offer. I still think deSoutier's tried to con us. And Simon Wells, he can't really know what Broadlands is worth, not as deSoutier does. But there's an edge between the pair of them. Let's use it. And if deSoutier gets screwed—either by losing, or paying more than he expected, that suits me fine. So, it's been decided —and on this one Tom Black did go along with me—that we'll hold an auction, they have thirty-six hours to put their packages together and we'll take the bidding at the Hilton. I want you there.'

'Why?'

'You're still my adviser. And this is crunch time. The board will be bringing in legal advisers but they're a cautious bunch—and new to the situation. You're not: you know my mind. I want you sitting in on the negotiations. On my behalf.'

'I'm not sure—'

'Why are you so bloody indecisive these days? Be there, at the Hilton. Wells and deSoutier are taking suites and they'll have their advisers with them. When the bids come in at nine-thirty a.m. I want you there to advise me. You'll do it.'

Eric hesitated. 'All right,' he said reluctantly. 'But let's get something clear. I can't spend any more time on this. Once the bid is accepted, I'm bowing out. There's an argument about conflict of interest—'

'Martin and Channing? I heard they're tying in with Corsa and deSoutier to provide some of the financing. I trust you, Eric. As far as I'm concerned, there's no problem of conflict.'

'Leonard Channing is pushing otherwise.'

'Just noise. You can handle that. OK, so I'll see you at the Hilton and—'

'One moment.' Eric paused, and the silence grew. It was as though she knew what he was about to say. 'You haven't asked me about my visit to Regent's Park.'

She made no reply.

'I've had a call from the police,' Eric went on. 'It wasn't a pleasant experience.'

'You used to be a copper yourself.'

He ignored the irrelevance. 'They checked me. Just to make sure I wasn't Cynthia Wishart's lover.'

'What?' She sniggered, but it was a nervous reaction triggered by tension. 'I did warn you about her.'

'This isn't funny, O'Hara. She's dead. And there's something about the death that I find . . . odd.'

'What?'

'Earlier . . . before she died. Her manner. The way she received me. Anyway . . . I tried to contact you after I'd seen her. Tried your flat and Broadlands. No trace. Where were you?'

'Hey, hold on, Ward! You're not my keeper! I don't need to explain my movements to you.' There was a sharpness in her voice but Eric felt it was feigned anger. 'As it happens,' she continued, 'I was out to dinner. With a friend. Anyway, what did the police have to say? Do they think the circumstances surrounding her death strange in any sense?'

'They haven't confided in me,' Eric said drily.

'And the tests?'

'I didn't bed her, O'Hara,' Eric said coldly.

'No. I guess not. After all, you would hardly have had time, would you? And now she's gone, maybe we'll never learn who her secret lover might have been. Still, enough of that. I've got business. I'll see you at the Hilton.'

After she rang off Eric sat quietly behind his desk, idly playing with the pencil in his hand. He stared at it, but didn't see it. He was thoughtful, and puzzled. Eileen O'Hara had sent him to see Cynthia Wishart because of a phone call. After the visit Eric hadn't been able to contact her. And now the woman was dead, Eileen O'Hara seemed to have no interest in the matter.

What was it she had said about the police suspicion that Eric had made love to Cynthia Wishart?

'. . . you would hardly have had time . . .'

She had not even asked Eric what information he might have got from Cynthia Wishart; she had not been concerned to know whether there was anything suspicious behind the management buy-out bid from Ted deSoutier.

After a while, with a degree of reluctance, he picked up the phone and called Phil Cooper. The financial journalist was at his desk.

'Ward! I'm glad you called. I've just had a session with a very angry man.'

'Ted deSoutier?'

'The very same.' Cooper chuckled. 'That woman

certainly knows how to put the boot in. Our friend deSoutier was certain he'd swing the board to his offer since he'd topped Wells, and I got the impression he's less than pleased with Andrew Strain. He'd lobbied him, is my guess, and maybe got a half promise. And the guy hasn't come through.'

'Tom Black and Hall Davies supported O'Hara.'

'Not in her own view, it seems. I gather she wanted to go for Wells, come hell or high water.'

'There's animosity between her and deSoutier.'

'Sex and business can be a fiery combination . . . yes, the gossip is around about. Anyway, I wanted a word, just to check that this auction thing is really on, and to let you know that my impression is deSoutier's really going to go for broke.'

'It's all becoming personal: they're an unholy trio,' Eric said bitterly. 'Wells, deSoutier and O'Hara, they all have scores to settle unconnected with the business in hand.'

'And what about this Wishart thing?'

Eric was silent for a while. 'I thought you were a *financial* journalist.'

'Come on, Ward, the newspaper world isn't *that* closed! I'm just curious . . . I mean, Broadlands seems to be very much in the wars these days, don't you agree? First, their company secretary gets mugged and killed; then the business is under a management buy-out proposal and a war starts; now, Mrs Wishart falls down stairs and breaks her neck. Could all be coincidental, of course—'

'She'd phoned Eileen O'Hara shortly before she died,' Eric said quietly.

There was a silence. After a while, Cooper said, 'The way that came out, you're telling me it wasn't a social call.'

'And this is confidential, and off the record, Cooper.'

'I hear you.'

Eric hesitated, not sure of the wisdom of continuing. 'Mrs Wishart phoned O'Hara to tell her she thought there was something odd going on behind the scenes in the leveraged buy-out.'

'The hell she did!' Cooper whistled softly. 'What was it?'

'Not explicit. That's why I was asked to go see her.'

'And you *went*? Bloody hell! What did you find?'

'Nothing. She said she'd just been seeking attention in her loneliness. There was nothing to her story.'

'You believe her?'

Eric hesitated. 'No. I don't think so. I got the impression she was . . . sort of talking to a prepared script in her mind. She had changed her attitude maybe; decided not to voice her suspicions. So I got nothing. Except the thought that she wasn't telling the truth . . . and that she was waiting for someone.'

'I don't quite follow . . .'

'She died in the early hours of the morning. A broken neck. Someone had been with her . . . slept with her . . . before she died.'

Cooper's breathing was slow and regular. 'What exactly are you driving at, Ward?'

'I really don't know. But if my impressions were valid, then there is a story she could have told me. I'd like to find out what it was.'

'I don't work for the crime page.'

'No. But I'm talking about business, and finance. She told O'Hara there was something behind the bid. She wouldn't come clean with me. Maybe you can find out what it was.'

Cooper was silent. 'Hmm . . . I can ask around. I'm owed some favours . . . And there's always been something slightly odd about Broadlands, over the last year or so.'

'In what way?'

'I think I've mentioned it to you before. Broadlands have been in the doldrums, and then deSoutier made his bid. That's fine, but in such a company, becalmed means little or no movement in share prices. But, oddly, they've been moving. Someone had confidence in Broadlands long before the market took interest in the leveraged buy-out bid.'

'The managers?'

'Neilson, Daly and deSoutier? I don't think so ... unless they use nominees. But why would they? Putting a financial package together would have been tough enough—and the idea was that they'd take control anyway. No, that doesn't make sense. No matter ... it's probably a red herring. Leave it with me. I'll get some feelers out.'

'Keep in touch.'

'I will. And enjoy yourself at the auction!'

3

The board members had all taken rooms in the Hilton, with a view over the park and two floors above the Wells contingent. Corsa had booked the floor above that for himself, deSoutier and the managers Neilson and Daly. Each group had been joined by dark-suited men, corporate lawyers and accountants who would be responsible for outlining the options and ensuring that their clients did not overstretch themselves, either in their financial commitments or in the strategy adopted in dealing with Broadlands. There was an air of expectancy in the hotel itself, even in the lobby, as though the staff were aware that decisions of consequence were being made, even if the hotel itself were not affected, and even though such occasions were not unique in the hotel's experience.

The meetings had commenced in the early evening.

Preliminary discussions had taken place between O'Hara, with Eric in attendance, and the Simon Wells contingent. Surprisingly, Wells himself took little part in the discussions. He remained hunched in his chair at the far end of the room, with an untouched glass of whisky in his hand, while his negotiators argued for him. Eric also had little to say: Eileen O'Hara was capable enough of sustaining an argument for herself, and as the bargaining went on he was able to sit back and watch, conscious of the growing respect the Wells negotiators began to develop for the woman facing them. O'Hara herself was animated: while Eric had always considered her desirable he would not, until now, have thought of her as beautiful, but as the excitement of the discussion took hold of her a new warmth came into her face and her eyes shone.

It had its impact upon the negotiators: he got the impression they could not forget she was a woman, and in some indefinable way it seemed to turn to her advantage in the discussions.

When they left the Wells contingent and met Pete Corsa the situation was different. Both Corsa and deSoutier took a central and active position in the discussions as guidelines were laid down. Neilson and Daly remained in the background as they had tended to do throughout, listening intently, making notes, and occasionally whispering between themselves, but leaving the negotiations and the front running largely to deSoutier. Ted deSoutier himself made no secret of the war that now lay openly between him and Eileen O'Hara. If Pete Corsa thought the obvious antagonism unwise he made no attempt to control it; Eric guessed the man had thought the issue through and decided there was more to be lost than gained by attempting to interfere in the personal battle between O'Hara and deSoutier. So the resentment simmered on, appearing in words and gestures, notably on deSoutier's part.

The meetings ended at nine-thirty with both groupings getting down to preparing their bids for the board in a long night session. A final dig was made at deSoutier with Eileen O'Hara, in front of her former lover, inviting Eric to her suite for a light supper. The thought clearly crossed deSoutier's mind that she might have had things other than business in view and his features darkened; Eric realized she could still demonstrate a certain power over the man's emotions. Later, as he and O'Hara were deeply involved in discussing the likely bids to come from the two groups Eric smiled to himself as he recalled his own thoughts that had briefly touched upon the same theme. He chided himself for his male egotism: romance was far from O'Hara's mind.

'So, what do you consider their relative positions might be?' she asked at last.

'As far as I can see, deSoutier will come in heavily with Corsa, and not far short of another hefty rise in the bid. They're terrified that Wells will take advantage of this auction to hike the price beyond Corsa's commitments—'

'Which is where banks like Martin and Channing, with their support for Corsa's package, will become important.'

Eric nodded. 'What we don't know is how far Wells will go. There's clearly a personality issue involved—'

Eileen O'Hara grunted. 'The thing about his ex-wife.'

'That's right. It sort of throws an unpredictable element into his reactions.'

She looked at him coolly. 'In the same way that it's all blood and guts for me and deSoutier?'

Eric shrugged. 'Now that you ask, I sometimes wonder whether any of this battle has to do with business, at its base.'

'Believe me, it does.' She took a deep breath and shook her head. 'The business is the thing . . . it's just that the whole thing has become sharpened by personal issues.'

'It certainly has with Simon Wells. But since he made no contribution to the discussion I wasn't able to fathom just how committed he is to seeing deSoutier down the drain. Have you heard who's backing his bid?'

Eileen O'Hara frowned. 'He's managed to keep those cards tight to his chest. There are rumours that it's American backed, but no names have come to light.'

'His background would suggest he'll be using a junk bond issue to support his package.'

'Do you think that's dangerous?' she asked. 'I mean, if

A NECESSARY DEALING

he puts in an inflated bid to see deSoutier out, and then his junk bond issue falls flat—'

'It's a point we'll need to raise, once the bids are in,' Eric replied. 'And if we're going to be able to get a sensible evaluation of the respective packages when the board meets, I need to spend some time on these preliminary papers from both parties.'

'And I've got to meet the board now,' she sighed. 'They'll have had their dinner and enjoyed their wine, so they should be receptive to my reports. It would have been better if they'd entered the early negotiations . . .'

'This was your idea, O'Hara,' Eric said, smiling slightly.

She looked at him and nodded. 'I guess so. But . . . it means there'll be little sleep for us tonight, Eric.'

There was an underlying note in her voice which suggested to him that she regretted they could not be spending time in a different manner.

It was almost two in the morning before Eric managed to complete a summary of the papers he had received on O'Hara's behalf from both parties to the auction. Even then, once he had stretched out on the bed there was a phone call from the Wells contingent, and he was forced to dress again, trail back to their suite and enter into some clarifications of the company situation with them. Simon Wells was still there, shirt-sleeved now, and the tousling of his hair suggested he had been rather more active in the discussions than he had been in front of Eric. The air-conditioning was going full blast, but the men were sweating, red-faced, as though there had been some plain talking. Eric was left with the impression there were elements of disagreement among the advisers—it could be that Wells was insisting upon forging ahead against their advice. When he got back to his room at three he decided not to bother getting undressed again, in case a call came from Corsa.

None came.

In any case, Eric was unable to sleep. His mind was full of numbers, figures juxtaposed with company reports, balance sheets with scribbled calculations, four year plans matched against performance indicators and targets. But after a while his thoughts drifted away from such mechanics to a four-in-the-morning hazy time when unreality took over, when fantasy stepped in, and he began to build images and pictures in his mind, enhanced by the darkness, and his insomnia, and the beginning of a prickle behind his eyes, the early signs of the kind of tension that could lead to pain.

He could envisage Cynthia Wishart's crumpled body lying in the stairwell of the Regent's Park flat, and he could see a dark figure leaping out to knife her husband, months earlier. And for what? To snatch a briefcase, it seemed—just a briefcase.

Muggers grabbed purses, demanded money . . . but did they often seize briefcases? What of value could be discovered inside a briefcase? Certainly not enough to pay for the mugger's addiction to drugs . . . and that was the police theory, it seemed, from what he had been told. A mugger, high on crack, trying to grab a briefcase. A struggle, Fred Wishart putting up an unwise resistance, and a knifing, a death in the dark street. Pointless, and unnecessary.

And yet early morning fantasies suggested perhaps it had not been pointless. Perhaps there had been purpose in the attack. Perhaps Cynthia Wishart had not fallen accidentally to her death.

She drank vodka; O'Hara had said so, and Eric had seen a half-empty bottle at the flat. Detective-Superintendent Mason had mentioned whisky. It could have been a slip of the tongue. Or maybe it had been her lover's drink.

It swirled around in his mind in the darkened room. A mugging; the theft of a briefcase; a phone call from the distraught widow months later; two deaths. Connections were lacking.

Unless the connection was the leveraged buy-out proposed by Ted deSoutier.

The man who had had an affair with Eileen O'Hara. A ladies' man. A man who would have had close dealings with Fred Wishart.

Someone had made love to Cynthia Wishart before she died.

At four in the morning everything could seem possible . . .

He dozed.

At seven he gave up the possibility of sleep, undressed, took a shower and shaved. In the mirror his eyes seemed pouched, dark-ringed, and there was a greyness about his skin that denoted tiredness. His eyes were sore. He took the precaution of using some pilocarpine.

He dressed again, and called from service for orange juice and coffee. When it arrived, the waiter was chatty but Eric remained monosyllabic in his responses. At seven-thirty he left the hotel and walked into the park. The traffic was heavy already, commuters pouring into the city. On the various floors in the Hilton the lawyers and accountants would be sweating away, putting the final touches to their packages for presentation to the Broadlands board. When he came back into the lobby and collected his key Eric was told there had been a telephone call for him. The message asked him to ring back: it was from Phil Cooper.

He took it in his room.

'Eric? Early morning stuff, but I thought you'd like to know. I've been doing some checking, as I promised, and the results are already coming in. You know it's dead easy these days to find out what share movements have been occurring, because the records are all computerized—one of the better results of Big Bang.'

'So?'

'So the sort of gut feelings I've been having about share movements are backed by the computer. There's been steady trading in Broadlands shares, going beyond normal interest for a company in the doldrums, and going back . . . oh . . . a good eight months.'

'Is that significant?'

'Early to say,' Cooper replied. 'But I've managed to pull off some names. None of them are well known to me—which means they're not deeply involved in the City. Some Midlands-based businessmen, Maxted, Arundel, Fraser . . . and one guy from your neck of the woods. Paulson.'

'Eddie Paulson?' Eric was stunned for a moment. 'I know him . . . I mean . . . well, let's say he's a little on the shady side—'

'Well, he took a hefty investment in Broadlands some eight months ago, and then dumped the shares back on the market about twelve weeks back.'

'He's hit problems financially,' Eric said grimly, thinking both of the Morcomb Estates suit and the racetrack.

'Well, he didn't do badly out of this deal. Assuming he took the money himself, of course.'

'How do you mean?' Eric asked.

Cooper's tone became guarded. 'I can't be specific, of course. But if you look at the purchasing patterns here over the last few months, and if you're really suspicious, you might consider that maybe there's a syndicate been set up to do the dealing. But there'd be only one reason for such a syndicate arrangement in secrecy.'

'And what's that?'

'The syndicate has to know something the general public doesn't.'

Eric considered the thought quietly for a few moments. Secret information; businessmen based in the Midlands and the North. 'You're talking about insider trading.'

'I'm saying I can see no reason for share trading of this kind to occur eight months ago, and going on steadily ever since, unless someone in the group knew something—and knew it before deSoutier put in his first proposal for the buy-out.'

'What could that be?'

'Your guess is as good as mine.'

'I'm not much good at guessing in this game.' A thought struck him suddenly. 'I don't suppose there's any Martin and Channing connection, is there?'

'You mean Leonard Channing, don't you?' Cooper laughed. 'I'm afraid not.'

'You'll keep at it?'

'Believe me, my journalistic nostrils are smelling something peculiar. I'll be keeping at it, for my own satisfaction as much as yours.'

At nine Eileen O'Hara rang him in his room, to suggest they met immediately, before the board was convened. He joined her in her suite, noting that she too had probably not slept well.

'I feel bloody awful,' she announced frankly. 'I couldn't get the business out of my mind. If that bastard deSoutier manages to persuade the board . . .'

'It was on my mind too,' Eric admitted. He hesitated. 'Tell me, while it's none of my business, why did you split up with deSoutier?'

She stared at him. 'It is none of your business. But . . .' She shrugged. 'I like to feel an element of . . . exclusivity in my sexual relationships. Ted deSoutier, well, he liked to play the field.'

'Did he ever get into the long grass with Cynthia Wishart?'

O'Hara's nose wrinkled in thought. 'The doll-like Cynthia? I wouldn't have thought she was deSoutier's type. Why do you ask?'

Eric shook his head. 'Just a thought that came to me in the reaches of the night.'

'You had nothing better to do?'

He looked at her. There was a slight smile on her lips and her eyes were bold. 'I think we'd better get to business,' he suggested.

They discussed the way in which she should handle the board meeting. The sealed bids would be made available to her as chairman at nine-thirty: they expected both parties to be ready. 'I gather,' she said drily, 'Andrew Strain, Hall Davies and Tom Black weren't allowed much sleep either. Tom rang me at eight: both the Corsa people and the Wells camp thought they'd better do some lobbying. Talking to me wasn't enough. Lawyers and accountants have been up and down those lifts like rabbits in and out burrows.'

'Any commitments?'

'Not according to Tom. Open minds all round, it seems—but I'll believe that when I see it happen on the Broadlands board.'

The meeting convened promptly at nine-thirty in the Broadlands suite.

The curtains remained drawn and the room was lit with a subdued light, as though to calm tempers and maintain a steadiness in a situation that could become heated and angry. Andrew Strain looked sharp; his ascetic features were as carefully assembled as usual, but there were high spots of colour in his cheeks that made Eric wonder whether he had fortified himself already this morning, in an attempt to stoke up his courage for the fray. Hall Davies was dressed in a light suit and seemed relaxed, easy in manner. He was smoking a pipe, teeth clenched on the stem, giving himself a sober, reflective air, but when he caught O'Hara's disapproving glance he tapped the bowl gently into the ashtray and then replaced the empty pipe between his teeth. He smiled mockingly at O'Hara, stroking his thick moustache, but she was staring at her papers. He winked conspiratorially in Eric's direction, a man accustomed to the whims of women and accustomed also to getting around them.

Tom Black was last to arrive. There was a strain about the edges of his mouth that served to remind Eric that everyone in this boardroom would probably have had a sleepless night, in view of the lobbying from the two camps — the would-be hedonist Strain, maybe even the thoughtful Hall Davies who as a salesman would be used to dissembling, and Tom Black himself. Eric caught himself watching the tanned features of Tom Black, the perpetual understudy who had once tried to get close to Eileen O'Hara and been rebuffed. He suddenly realized that there was never very much to read in Tom Black's eyes. The man kept his feelings in strict reserve.

John Leslie, the company secretary, coughed meaningfully, and Eileen O'Hara opened the meeting.

'We have but the one item on the agenda for this meeting. In view of the nature of declared interests in that item I informed deSoutier, Neilson and Daly that they should not be present for the item, other than as presenters of their bid. They have agreed to remain outside the meeting. Before we deal with the matters in hand, however, is there any general comment anyone would wish to make?'

Andrew Strain leaned forward, his accountant's eyes gleaming coldly. 'Just one comment, Madam Chairman. I trust that the matter will be *resolved* today. I make the point bearing in mind the last fiasco. We could have settled issues then, and in my view should have done. There was a clear bid on the table—'

'We've been over this, Andrew,' O'Hara snapped.

'We have,' Tom Black intervened, 'at the last board meeting. But I must say I agree with Andrew. I think we could cause damage to the company if we protract this matter beyond today. We don't want a repetition of the uncertainties last time. Personal issues crept in—'

'The deSoutier bid was dishonest!' Eileen O'Hara insisted. 'While there is personal animosity between us, which I admit to, I was thinking of the company—'

'As we all are,' Hall Davies interrupted. 'But I too agree. We must settle the matter once and for all today. You'll have seen how unsettled share prices have become in the wake of this management bid: all right, they've risen steadily, but there was a tremor last time, and if we should experience any further indecisiveness it could lead to a market loss of confidence in our shares—'

'I think the point is made . . . and taken,' O'Hara said, glaring around at the members of her board. 'So shall we get on?'

'I understand,' John Leslie remarked, 'we can take the presentation of Mr Wells first. He has intimated his team are ready.'

Eileen O'Hara glanced around the table to take the meeting's assent. Each man nodded in turn. 'Fine,' she said, with a sigh. 'Then let's do battle.'

In the hour that followed Simon Wells followed the pattern of behaviour demonstrated in his own suite, when O'Hara and Eric had gone through the negotiations with his team. He remained aloof, sitting with his chair well back from the table, his eyes hooded, seemingly indifferent to the presentation his team was making on his behalf, and uninterested in the reaction of the board to his offer.

The lawyers droned on. Eric, already familiar with the structure of the bid, found his attention wandering. He watched Wells curiously: the flash of passion he had detected in the man when they had first met seemed now to have been brought under control. There was no doubt in Eric's mind that the advice Wells had been getting was that he was pushing things too far in his personal vendetta against Pete Corsa; equally, there was nothing to suggest to Eric that the arbitrageur was taking that advice seriously. And when the lawyers made their final statements Wells remained impassive.

'Those are the details of the offer,' Wells's adviser stated. 'It amounts, when all is taken into account, to a bid that is worth, on today's terms, some thirty-nine million.'

Eric glanced quickly around the faces of the board members. All remained impassive, with the exception of Hall Davies: a nervous tic had developed in his left cheek. Self-consciously he put his hand up, above his moustache, as though to steady the tremor.

There was a short pause. Then Eileen O'Hara inclined her head. 'Thank you, gentlemen. We hope to make an announcement today.'

Wells was first to rise to his feet. He stared at O'Hara, his eyes blurred, as though he seemed vaguely dazed. He could hardly have expected a clear reaction from the board before deSoutier's bid came in for consideration, yet now his cards had been played he seemed reluctant to leave. One of his advisers took his arm; he shook it off in a petulant gesture, and then led the group from the room, silently.

After the door closed, Andrew Strain let out a long, pent-up sigh. He glared challengingly at O'Hara. 'At thirty-nine million,' he announced harshly, 'Simon Wells hasn't even matched deSoutier's last bid. Just what is the point in all this, O'Hara? This could have been settled without all this performance.'

'We'd better hear from the managers,' she replied stonily.

Coffee was served. The conversation was strained, Black and Hall Davies talking about golfing matters while Andrew Strain reminded Eric he was an old acquaintance of Leonard Channing's. There was a cunning note in Strain's voice, as though he was hinting he knew all about the pressure Channing was putting on Eric, but no comment about conflict of interest was made.

The in-house phone rang. Leslie took it and nodded. 'They're ready,' he said. The board meeting was reconvened.

Ted deSoutier marched in, his jaw set aggressively, ready for a fight. Neilson and Daly were with him, looking serious. No one else entered with them. O'Hara raised her eyebrows.

'The rest of your party?'

Ted deSoutier sat down, and motioned to the other two

managers to do likewise. 'I've dispensed with our advisers,' he announced. 'We know our bid; Pete Corsa is happy to leave things to me. The papers are here and you can see them, but we've now revised our strategy, the one we put to you and Ward late last night. Basically, we've decided to stand pat on our bid, as far as the general terms are concerned. With two exceptions.'

O'Hara straightened in her chair. 'The exceptions?'

'First, we're prepared to raise our bid. Significantly. But there's a proviso—it's the second difference from our original bid.'

Her tone was icy; Eric suspected she was guessing what was coming. 'The proviso?'

'We want you out of the chair: a vote of no confidence in your handling of this situation.'

There was a long silence. The members of the board seemed thunderstruck. Constitutionally, they would find it difficult to force such an issue through: O'Hara held a large shareholding in Broadlands. On the other hand, without the support of her board life would be difficult, if not impossible if she remained in the chair.

She looked around at her fellow directors: none looked at her. They seemed to be frozen, staring at deSoutier's arrogant mouth. If she had expected an instant clamour of protest from the directors, she was disappointed. 'All right,' O Hara said contemptuously, 'I think the best plan will be to see whether we have any basis at all for deliberation. You say you're prepared to raise the bid.'

'Provided you vacate the chair,' deSoutier repeated.

'I think the board understands that. Be kind enough to let us know just what you propose ... in your raising the offer.'

Ted deSoutier stared at her triumphantly. 'I believe it's a bid this board can't resist. Whatever Wells has put in is suspect: he's ruled by ideas of vengeance, and has lost sight of reality. I haven't. With Pete Corsa, and the backing of certain merchant banks like Martin and Channing, and Delafield, our package is solid—and not financed by junk bonds.'

'The bid, deSoutier,' O'Hara said, injecting weariness into her voice.

'Forty-two million,' deSoutier said with a cynical smile. Someone gasped.

'You can't raise that,' O'Hara snapped.

'It's in the bag—and you're out of the chair,' deSoutier retorted. His triumphant glance swept the room. 'Can anyone here suggest you can afford to turn us down?'

O'Hara's chair scraped noisily backwards. She stood up, knuckles on the table. Her already swarthy features had darkened. '*I* can! I don't trust you, deSoutier. This bid is way ahead of your original offer, and my views haven't changed! My vote will be cast to turn this offer down—'

'Now hold on,' Andrew Strain expostulated.

Tom Black was rising to his feet also. His eyes were excited, and he was shaking his head. 'Eileen, you can't—'

Ted deSoutier forestalled him. 'As members of this board I, Neilson and Daly demand we be allowed to make representations, having declared our interest, and go through our bid in detail. We're acting in the interests of the board and the company, and I insist you can't allow the whims of a woman to overrule common sense.'

'Insist? You can insist on damn-all while I'm in the chair. I'm adjourning the meeting forthwith!' O'Hara almost shouted.

'And I'm challenging that adjournment!' deSoutier yelled, slamming his fist on the table. 'It's time we stopped being dragged along in this way, just because your old man left you a chunk of shares! This is the business world. I want a vote taken—'

'We have only one item of business in this meeting and the issue of my chairmanship isn't it! You're out of order!'

'Then I demand a special meeting of the board to debate the matter!'

Eric could see John Leslie, the company secretary, red in the face, unable to decide which way he should advise his chairman to react. But as far as Eric could see the matter was already beyond redemption. O'Hara was determined on a course of action; there was no stopping her. Ted deSoutier's bid might be larger than Wells's but she would never accede to it—particularly now he had added the proviso for its acceptance. It was a direct challenge to her authority over the board: an appeal to their cupidity, and a demand that they withdraw their support from her.

'This meeting is adjourned,' she announced icily.

But from the silence that greeted her decision it was clear that the matter was far from concluded.

4

The reaction of the City to the news was almost immediate. While deSoutier, with Corsa's backing, and Simon Wells had been matching bids the effect upon Broadland shares had been clear; a steady rise, reflecting the interest the City always took in a management buy-out with its promises of riches to come. The boardroom battle was another matter entirely: it placed issues in doubt, it sparked off uncertainties, and there was an immediate panic selling as profits were taken by the nervous among the investors. While the price steadied after a day or so, it still remained shaky and even after Tom Black was interviewed by the financial press there was little confidence in the market place for Broadlands shares.

'The fact is,' Phil Cooper confided over the telephone to Eric in Newcastle, 'the City feels that O'Hara is taking an unwise stand. Ted deSoutier's bid is far and away the better one, and Wells's financing is based on a junk bond issue—he's not got the merchant banks like Martin and Channing behind him. So the analysts favour deSoutier's bid. And they feel O'Hara's being . . . female.'

'What about Tom Black's statement to the Press?'

'Yeah.' Cooper breathed thoughtfully. 'Interesting, isn't it? While it was ostensibly calculated to defuse the situation and calm the anxious, there was more than a hint in it of Black's own ambitions. He was certainly not going along with O'Hara's stand. Looks to me like the deputy is deserting his chairman at long last. I sat in on the briefing, you know. He was terse, kinda tense, but very clear in what he was saying. Special notice of a board meeting has been given, because O'Hara is refusing to reconvene the adjourned meeting. There was no doubt among the financial journalists present about what Black and the others have in mind. They are going for her jugular because she's allowing personal interests to supersede business sense. They'll be demanding she put the deSoutier offer to the vote, or else vacate the chair.'

'She holds a large shareholding—'

'But with no board to support her, she'll be dead. No, she'll have to go, if she doesn't back down over deSoutier.'

'She's still being adamant.'

'You're her adviser.'

'There's certain advice she won't take.' Eric hesitated. 'Have you picked up any further information about the Cynthia Wishart thing?'

There was a short silence. 'I can't be certain,' Cooper said slowly, 'but the crime desk certainly has the feeling there's a suspicion around that maybe she didn't fall, she was pushed . . . but there's little to go on, and the boys in blue are keeping their heads well down so far. Pursuing their inquiries, as they say . . .'

'And the consortium?'

'Still working on it. I've got confirmation of the Midlands people involved, and your northern wheeler-dealer Paulson is also confirmed as having bought in and then sold out a few months back, but what I haven't been able to discover is who set the deal up. The parties, naturally, aren't talking, but there's certainly been a cover-up of the trail. It'll take a hell of a lot of digging up, with shell companies and offshore trusts being used to shade over the dealings . . . the sort of thing you might never get the truth out of.'

'You'll keep working at it?' Eric asked.

'As long as there's a story in it.'

When he replaced the receiver, Eric felt unsettled. Eileen O'Hara had been in touch the previous day, and although he had tried to persuade her she was fighting a losing battle she had been adamant in her refusal to deal with deSoutier: the old wound was scored too deeply. Yet she did not refer to it; rather, she insisted she felt instinctively there was something wrong with the bid, deSoutier had moved too high, too easily, such a long distance from his original bid.

Eric was inclined to agree, but instinct was not enough.

He thought about it for another twenty-four hours before he phoned Charles Davison and fixed an appointment with the solicitor. He insisted the meeting be held at Davison's offices.

By comparison with the Quayside, they were palatial.

They took up a large part of the ground floor of a modern office block: Eric noted that the owners of the block were identified in a holding company which Eric knew was largely in the hands of Davison himself. It made him wonder why the man should descend to ripping off Eddie Paulson for a hundred and fifty thousand and risk his reputation—what reputation he had among his fellow professionals. He guessed it would be almost like a gut reaction: Davison could not resist the opportunity. Taking that kind of risk would be an automatic reaction, a gambler at the tables.

Eric sat impassively in the deep leather chair in the waiting-room and stared at the elegant décor, the expensive pictures, and was aware of the even more expensive receptionist behind her rosewood desk. He had guessed he would have to wait: Charles Davison would regard it as important, a small reminder of the difference in their professional status and perception of themselves, to keep him waiting.

'Mr Davison will see you now.'

She had no trace of a Tyneside accent and her eyes were empty and bored.

In his office, Davison made no attempt to rise as Eric entered. He was shirtsleeved, at ease; his chair leaned back as he lolled behind a clean-surfaced, leather-finished desk, and he had the air of a confident man, certain that his way was the right way. His surroundings confirmed him in that impression each day.

'So, Ward, you've reached a decision.' Davison waved a patronizing hand in Eric's direction. 'Take a seat.'

Eric did so, leaning back casually. 'That's right, I've decided what to do.'

'As I . . . requested?'

'More or less.'

Davison was not sure he liked the evasiveness of the answer. He frowned slightly. 'We do understand each other, I hope.'

'Precisely,' Eric replied. 'You conned Eddie Paulson into giving you that money by persuading him you, and only you, could swing the Morcomb Estates deal—even though you were acting for Morcomb on retainer, and knew that it was a settlement Morcomb would go for in any event.'

Davison smiled thinly, and glanced around the room. 'We're not bugged here, Ward, so carry on.'

'Paulson's suit for the return of the money and an accounting for profits earned is embarrassing to you, but maybe I can help you. I've looked up the law, and there's an interpretation we can put on it . . .'

'One the other side can accept, without going to court?'

'Maybe.'

'It would,' Davison said slowly, 'be better that way.'

'Who's acting for Paulson?'

'Donald Enderby.'

'I know him.'

'A reasonable man?'

'Reasonable enough.' Eric paused. 'And he trusts me.'

Charles Davison was silent for a few moments. He stared at Eric, frowning thoughtfully, clearly puzzled at Eric's attitude. He had threatened that if Eric failed to support him, he would bring Anne Ward and Morcomb Estates into disrepute by association, and now he did not trust Eric's seeming compliance.

'I have a feeling,' he said at last, 'you want something from me.'

'That's right.'

Davison brought his chair to an upright position. He leaned forward, elbows on the desk in front of him, his handsome face now scarred with suspicion. He had thought he might have trouble persuading Eric to act for him and consequently had used the crude approach at the Quayside. Now, he was puzzled. 'So tell me. What is it you want?'

'Access to Eddie Paulson's financial affairs.'

Charles Davison seemed almost stunned for a while. There was a long silence. Davison stared at Eric uncomprehendingly, as though he could hardly believe what he had heard. Then a wolfish grin spread across his mouth, tentative, but sneering. 'Well, I'm damned! So the incorruptible bloody Ward is as dirty as the rest of us after all!'

Eric's face was stony. He made no reply, but there was an unpleasant taste in his mouth.

Davison stood up and thrust his hands deep in his trouser pockets, walked around the desk and stood in front of Eric. 'So let's get this right. You'll act for me, make your best endeavours on my behalf, in return for access to information I probably don't have anyway?'

'You'll have it. Or you'll know where to get it,' Eric replied.

'But why should I even try? I placed a choice upon your table—'

'I don't push easily, Davison,' Eric cut in coldly. 'You may have thought you could use that stupid threat to get me to act for you, but it wouldn't have worked. I'd have taken the chance with my wife's reputation—and I'd have acted for her on this occasion if you'd started slinging mud.'

'But things are different now, because you want something from me?'

'That's about the size of it.'

'*Quid pro quo*,' Davison said thoughtfully. He leaned back, thighs braced against his desk and regarded Eric owlishly. 'Well, I have to admit, I've always preferred dealing with a corrupt man rather than a straight one. You know where you stand. But I'd never expected to see you in that character part.'

'Let's just say it's a matter of means and ends, and leave it at that,' Eric replied.

Davison was silent for a while, and then he nodded slowly. 'All right, let's say that. This is something I can go along with. But Paulson's financial affairs . . . that's a tall order, and a complicated one. What exactly do you want to know?'

'It's fairly simple. He entered a transaction with a share-purchasing consortium. I know their names . . . or most of them. The name I lack is the person who set up the deals. I want nothing more than that. Just a name.'

'Share buying?' Davison wrinkled his nose. 'I don't recall anything of any great consequence . . . Paulson doesn't seem to have been much of a gambler in that direction. The horses, now—'

'He's been involved,' Eric said shortly.

Davison took a deep breath. 'I don't know that I can help. My dealings with Paulson have been over the settlement—'

'Rubbish. You've acted for him for years. It's common knowledge. The reason why you were able to persuade him into the Morcomb settlement in the first instance, and get him to believe you, is that he knows you're as crooked as he is from your past dealings together.'

'You need to watch your mouth, Ward.'

'I don't need advice from a man in your situation, Davison.'

Davison nodded slowly, his cold eyes never leaving Eric's face. Then finally he stood upright, as though he had taken a decision. He pressed the intercom button on his desk. 'Sheila? A coffee for my professional guest here.' He looked at Eric and nodded. 'OK. Wait here. I might be a while.'

He left the room before the coffee arrived.

Davison was away for more than half an hour. When he finally returned he was carrying a brown folder. He stood staring at Eric for a few moments and then he said, 'I can't let this leave the office.'

'I understand that.'

'There's nothing illegal in this file.'

'I didn't say there would be.'

Davison hesitated. 'So why do you want the information?' When Eric made no reply, he went on nervously, 'We have a deal?'

Eric didn't like saying it, but he nodded. 'We have a deal.'

Davison handed Eric the file. It contained perhaps twenty sheets of paper. Eric ran through them quickly. They dealt with Paulson's shareholdings of recent years. He had moved in and out of various holdings in a somewhat haphazard manner, it seemed, but always in significant sums. Towards the back of the file a name caught Eric's attention. Maxted, One of the names mentioned by Phil Cooper in relation to the West Midlands consortium. He read on more carefully.

Then he stopped, puzzled.

He closed the file, and handed it back to Davison, wordlessly.

'You got what you wanted?' Davison asked.

'Maybe,' Eric replied, and rose to leave. He wanted to

spend no more time than he needed to with Charles Davison.

Eric phoned Phil Cooper at his flat that evening. It was almost midnight before he finally made contact; Cooper had just got in and he sounded weary.

'All hell's broken loose over the Takeover Panel's decision on the Heald-Pemberton merger,' Cooper explained, 'and I had to get across to Paris for an interview, then back here to make a deadline . . . God, who'd be a financial journalist!'

'I thought it was all wine and roses.'

'It's not even *wife* and roses,' Cooper snorted. 'You know I've never even had time to get married? Anyway, I'm glad you called. Even though I've been up to my elegant hocks in Takeover Panel business I have not been idle on your behalf. I've had a couple of people out doing a scan of Broadlands, deSoutier, Neilson and Daly. Some interesting facts have emerged. Did you know, for instance, that friend Daly has an engineering background?'

'Is that significant?'

'Did you know that he was headhunted by deSoutier from a Japanese container shipping company?'

'I did not.'

'And were you aware that Neilson and Daly slipped off to Yokohama a year ago, during a leave period from the company?'

'That fascinating information had escaped me,' Eric replied patiently. 'I'm sure you have something to add.'

'I do indeed,' Cooper announced grimly. 'You see, there's some credibility to be given to the belief in certain business circles that the faceless Neilson and Daly, who have kept very low profiles in this deSoutier bid, have in fact been wriggling fingers very deep in the pie.'

'I don't understand.'

'Ted deSoutier is managing director and main front man, but something odd's been going on behind the scenes.'

'Such as?'

'Contracts.'

Eric was silent for a while. Phil Cooper's breathing had a satisfied sound to it. 'What sort of contracts?'

'The whisper is that Daly used his contacts to pull a deal with someone in Japan to haul in a container shipping service deal.'

'For Broadlands? But that's way outside its business interests—'

'Diversification, old son, diversification. And there's more: solid fuel and oil distribution contracts.'

'I've seen nothing in company reports issued by Broadlands—'

'Exactly.'

Both men were silent for a while. Eric took a deep breath. 'These contracts have not been disclosed to the board.'

'That's what I'm saying,' Cooper replied. 'But as far as the other business is concerned, I've been so busy chasing across to Paris and God knows where else that I've not been able to push further on this share-buying consortium thing. So I'm afraid I've got no further names.'

'I have,' Eric said quietly. 'I have.'

CHAPTER 6

1

'I'm glad you were able to come.'

Eric stared at Eileen O'Hara. She seemed to have lost much of the confidence that she had displayed when first they met: there were lines around her mouth and her dark skin had a greyish look as though she had not been sleeping well. He had made no attempt to contact her since the special meeting of the board had been called on petition;

she had rung him merely to ask if he would be there. She had not demanded his presence, merely asked, as though seeking information. He was left with the impression that much of the fight was going out of her: she was unable to face up to the consequences of losing the battle with deSoutier, and now, with the rest of her board. He was vaguely surprised—he had thought she was made of sterner steel. Or maybe it was just that she was a realist, because the odds were stacked against her.

The meeting was convened in the boardroom of Broadlands and Eileen O'Hara took the chair. The meeting was fully attended but everyone seemed to be busy with their eyes, concentrating upon their own affairs. Andrew Strain was reading his papers, Tom Black inspecting his pen, Neilson and Daly checking that their fingernails were still there, Hall Davies busy with a fly crawling across the table in front of him. Only Ted deSoutier seemed still prepared to register his position: he sat upright in his chair, staring fixedly at Eileen O'Hara. She held his glance for a while, then looked away as the company secretary called their attention to the business by announcing the special nature of the meeting.

'There are two items on the agenda. The first places a recommendation on record that the bid of Mr deSoutier and his colleagues by way of a management buy-out be approved; the second calls for a vote of no confidence in the chairman of the board.'

Eileen O'Hara's chin came up defiantly. 'All right, let's take the first of the two items. I'll take the chairman's privilege of speaking first on the issue. I am totally against acceptance of the bid made by Mr deSoutier. There are some of you who believe this is an emotional matter; I'm prepared to accept that there are emotional issues involved, but these are not the basic anxieties that gnaw at me. Rather, it is a simple matter of trust. I do not trust Mr deSoutier.'

Andrew Strain shuffled uneasily in his seat and cast a swift glance in O'Hara's direction as though wishing to protest. She looked at him, and he subsided.

'You may well ask,' she went on, 'why I do not trust deSoutier and this bid. I will admit he has helped this company during the last three years to a healthier position in the market place. But recent events have caused me to wonder just what is going on. The managers made an evaluation of this company and placed a bid before us. It might have been one we would have accepted, but Fate, in the shape of Simon Wells stepped in. He has a personal grudge against deSoutier's backer, and made a counter-bid through Hall Davies. Suddenly, and surprisingly, deSoutier is prepared to raise his offer significantly. And when further pressure comes on, up goes the bid again! Is this based upon a true valuation of the company? If it is, was the first bid from deSoutier an attempt to con us and the other shareholders? And if so, can we entrust the future of Broadlands to deSoutier? I say not: the margin between the first and the last bids is too great for me to believe we are still not being conned. I state from the chair, therefore: my vote will be against the deSoutier bid. I wish to take the bid from Simon Wells.'

'Supported by a junk bond issue?' Andrew Strain protested. 'O'Hara, you've got it wrong.'

'Which I suppose is a vote in favour of deSoutier,' she snapped.

'Since we're all talking freely today, I hope, let me put my views on the table. I think you've taken the wrong tack on these bids. All right, deSoutier got it wrong first time. But that was caution. And remember, he didn't have the advantage of the financial advice he's since taken, when he launched the first bid. As trust, do you really think we should trust Simon Wells?' Andrew Strain's eyes glittered. 'This is a vendetta between him and Corsa—we're just pawns. He has no interest in Broadlands *per se*. That's why my vote will go for deSoutier.'

There was a short silence. Ted deSoutier's head turned, so that he was staring directly at Hall Davies. The ex-sales director had been the man who had introduced the Wells bid in the first place. The handsome face was now strained, his mouth indecisive. 'This has been going on too long,' he intoned. 'The Wells bid is the better one . . . and I don't go along with Andrew's anxieties about the nature of the financial support. Junk bonds have had a bad press of late but they are still viable, and legal, and Wells is no fool: he might strip some assets out of Broadlands but that could result in a fitter, leaner company. At this stage I'm inclined to vote against deSoutier, and with our chairman . . . but I'd like to hear from Tom Black, first.'

Eileen O'Hara's eyes were glazed. Eric guessed she had been counting upon the support of Hall Davies. With deSoutier, Neilson and Daly declaring an interest in the proceedings they would be denied a vote by the board; that left Strain, Hall Davies and Tom Black as voting directors with O'Hara. Since his press release earlier in the week Black's loyalty was in doubt. So the voting could tie—Strain and Black against Hall Davies and O'Hara. But the chairman had a casting vote—O'Hara could swing the day with that second, casting vote.

But it presupposed Hall Davies's support. She looked at Tom Black. Eric wondered if she was now regretting past slights, for if she lost this vote, it was inevitable she would also lose chairmanship of Broadlands in addition.

'For my part,' Tom Black announced, 'I'm thinking only of the company. If we go back a few years we can remember the doldrums that followed Eileen's taking over Broadlands, after her father's death. Not her fault, but a fact, nevertheless —it's the way the City reacts to any change. We then saw under deSoutier's generalship a steadying, a recovery— even though we reached a certain plateau. And now, more recently, as news of the bid got out, we've seen a rapid surge in market interest in Broadlands stock. But now it's at risk.'

He paused, and looked around at his fellow members of the board. 'It's at risk because we've entered a damaging, bruising battle where decisions are not being taken quickly enough. It's a process of attrition, and the City recognizes the stalemate that's developing. The situation has to be resolved. Today.'

'I go with that,' Andrew Strain rumbled.

'But the resolution must be taken,' Black continued, 'not just to stop the present slide in share prices for Broadlands. The future of the company is at stake. And I have a view about that. I agree with Andrew; Wells will strip the guts out of this company, because he's basically not interested in it. He simply wants to beat Corsa. Is that a rational business decision? A rational way to invest? And we know damned well even his own financial advisers don't agree with what he's doing.'

Eric stared at the deputy chairman in surprise at the admission he had made.

'How do you know that, Tom?' Eileen O'Hara asked coldly.

He met her glance without flinching. 'Come on, Eileen, we were all lobbied at the Hilton, and you know it. More than that, the signs were all there. Wells is pushing against the advice of his own financial backers. It's a recipe for disaster, as far as Broadlands is concerned. So my view is this. Short term, we're in trouble unless we resolve the issue before us. Long term, we're without a real future if Simon Wells is successful. So whether Ted deSoutier got it wrong first time or not, the fact is his market valuation now is about right—and maybe even a bit better than we might expect. After all, Wells hasn't matched his bid. So, I think we have no logical choice other than the one I'm going for.'

'deSoutier?' O'Hara asked harshly.

'That's right. My regrets, Eileen, but it's got to be the management buy-out, for me.'

There was a short silence. Eileen O'Hara turned her head slowly to look around the boardroom table. Neilson and Daly kept their faces impassive but were unable to hide the excitement in their eyes; deSoutier was smiling slightly, a wolfish baring of the teeth.

'Time to vote, O'Hara.'

It was all down to Hall Davies, and they knew it. The man was staring at Tom Black, still trying to make up his mind. Then he shrugged, and looked down at his hands.

'The vote, O'Hara,' deSoutier repeated.

She gritted her teeth. 'The resolution to be voted upon calls for an acceptance of the management buy-out by deSoutier, Daly and Neilson. I will ask first for those in favour to so signify, so that it may be recorded by the company secretary. I'll begin with my deputy chairman.' She did not look at him, but stared straight down the table. 'Mr Black?'

'*For* the resolution.'

'Mr Strain?'

'I also vote for the resolution in the belief it is best for the company.'

'Hall Davies?'

He tried to look at her, but couldn't. 'The hell with it,' he said. 'Tom Black talks a lot of sense. The sentiments expressed from the chair . . . I go along with them, but we have to look at the present share prices, and determine what's best for the company in the future.' He shrugged. 'I vote for acceptance of the deSoutier bid.'

Eileen O'Hara stared at him for several seconds. Her mouth was stiff; she knew she had lost, but she was unwilling to reveal her true feelings. She needed a few seconds to gather herself and her emotions. Ted deSoutier was unwilling to allow her that time. 'You need to cast your own vote, O'Hara. The market would prefer the decision to be unanimous, of course.'

It was a brutal challenge, unnecessary but deliberate. She was defeated; he wanted her complete surrender. Some of the life came back into her eyes as she glared at him. 'You can go to hell, deSoutier. This decision will not be unanimous. I'm casting my vote against the resolution.'

'Makes little difference.' DeSoutier shrugged indifferently. 'The company secretary can record your vote. And that means you can now formally declare the resolution passed and we can move on to the next business—the vote of confidence in the chairman.'

'*One moment.*'

Tom Black raised his head to stare at Eric.

'I have no status here, but may I be permitted to speak?'

Andrew Strain's nose twitched, as though sniffing the wind for trouble. Eileen O'Hara looked around at the members of the board. Ted deSoutier shook his head; the others merely seemed startled.

'Are there any objections?' O'Hara asked.

'I object,' deSoutier announced. 'The matter is concluded; let's get on to next business.'

'Like Mr Ward,' O'Hara said acidly, 'you have no right to speak on this issue—until it is concluded. And I have not made any formal announcement. So, unless there is objection I propose to use chairman's privilege and allow Mr Ward to speak.'

They were nervous; Eric could feel it. Yet none was prepared to object, now the main battle was won. Eileen O'Hara nodded to him.

'I think it necessary to ensure that before a decision is finally recorded in the minutes, all relevant facts are placed before the board,' Eric said. 'Had the vote been against the resolution I would merely have spoken privately to Miss O'Hara, in the capacity of her adviser. She could then have taken such action she deemed proper. Now it seems to be a positive vote for the resolution. I feel I have to advise her publicly . . . and ensure the board also has the facts before it, in making its decision.'

'Facts?' Andrew Strain grated. 'What facts?'

'There has been some concern at the board regarding the difference between the first bid made by Mr deSoutier and the later ones. I believe there is good reason for that discrepancy: the later bids more nearly reflect the true value of the company, bearing in mind its prospects for the future. It is still, possibly, an undervaluation, however.'

Hall Davies leaned forward and cleared his throat. 'Prospects? I don't understand what you're driving at.'

'Contracts,' Eric replied. 'Contracts that have not been disclosed to the board.'

There was a long, stunned, silence. Ted deSoutier was staring at Eric, thunderstruck. He opened his mouth as though he were about to speak; then he thought better of it. He glanced in the direction of his two managers. It was Neilson who found the nerve to say something. 'I . . . I don't know what Mr Ward is talking about . . . I can vouch for the fact that there are no contracts that need to be disclosed. No such contracts exist.'

Eric smiled. 'Forgive me. An unpardonable omission for a lawyer. I should not have used the word *contracts* . . . rather I should have spoken of current negotiations.'

Tom Black cleared his throat. 'O'Hara, what is this? What's going on?'

'I don't know,' she said thoughtfully, her eyes fixed on Eric. 'I haven't had time to talk to Mr Ward recently. Perhaps I should have done.'

'There are no contracts,' Neilson insisted.

'But I have information which suggests,' Eric replied, 'that as long as eighteen months ago negotiations were begun in Japan over shipping container service contracts. I've also been told that the managers have been discussing service contracts in solid fuel and oil distribution. Now if this is truly the case, and if those contracts are likely to fall to Broadlands, it means that significant diversification possibilities arise. We are all aware that the company has suffered from an image which is . . . old-fashioned and boring. Its product range has been too limited. Mr deSoutier himself is of this opinion, I understand.'

'I don't see what this has to do—'

Eileen O'Hara stopped deSoutier's interruption with a raised hand. Suddenly, her authority seemed to have returned. 'Go on, Mr Ward.'

'If negotiations such as those I've mentioned have been under way, it may be questioned why the managers did not place the matter before the board. The matter of their *duty* to do so is irrelevant; they are also directors of the company, and as such they are under a legal duty to inform the board. Inevitably, such information, if released to the market, would give rise to a significant increase in share prices. But it seems the negotiations have not been disclosed to the board—'

'Instead,' Eileen O'Hara interrupted grimly, 'we had a proposal for a management buy-out. And at a low figure, at that!'

Neilson sat back in his chair. His face was ashen. The directors seemed to focus their attention upon him alone.

'Is there anything more?' Hall Davies asked. He sounded angry; Eric guessed his anger was directed as much at his own foolishness a few minutes ago in feeling he had been trapped at the last moment into a decision that had been against his basic inclinations.

Eric shrugged. 'I'm not sure. In a sense, I'm merely reporting as an adviser to Miss O'Hara. But now the board is aware that negotiations have been going on, the members may feel they would wish to question the managers—who are also directors—why disclosure was not made at the time their management buy-out bid was put forward to the Broadlands directors. They declared an interest, properly;

they did not, it seems, give full disclosure of secret information.'

'You *bastards*!' Hall Davies exploded. 'You bloody well tried to take us for a ride!'

Ted deSoutier was silent, his eyes hooded. Neilson's head was down, mouth working nervously. Daly was pale, his hands shaking, his eyes fixed on Ted deSoutier. Eileen O'Hara stared at the three of them bitterly. 'The question in my own mind is—did Pete Corsa know, also, what this board did not?'

There was no reply from deSoutier; his brows were knitted, deep in desperate thought. O'Hara's mouth twisted. 'I think I would wish to put the resolution to the board again, in view of what Mr Ward has said.'

'Facts . . .' Andrew Strain said nervously. 'Are these *really* facts, or guesses?'

'Even if they are just rumours,' O'Hara insisted, 'they need investigating before we take a decision on the buy-out.' She paused icily.' Tom?'

He didn't like it, and his mouth was stiff, but he nodded. 'I agree.'

'I hardly feel we need to take a formal vote,' O'Hara said sarcastically. 'The resolution can lie on the table, until we learn more about these negotiations that have been going on behind our backs.' She smiled tigerishly. 'And may I presume, also, that we can leave in abeyance the second resolution also?'

Ted deSoutier raised his head defiantly. For a moment he seemed on the point of challenging her, but realized he was unlikely to get support. He looked down at his hands, his mouth set hard in resentment and anger.

'In that case—'

'Please,' Eric said. 'May I make one more point?'

She looked at him; her eyes held a triumphant glow. 'I'm listening, Mr Ward.'

'Before further investigations are made, and before a

further board meeting is convened, it might be as well if all board members were given the opportunity to declare any interest any one of them might have had in these negotiations.'

They stared at him as if he had lost his senses.

'Are you suggesting one of *us* was involved in the negotiations?' Tom Black exploded.

'Or failing that,' Eric added, ignoring him, 'if any of them actually had *knowledge* of the contractual negotiations.'

There was a long, charged silence. Ted deSoutier was staring at him; there were dark shadows of calculation in his eyes as though he had suddenly decided Eric Ward was a dangerous man. Eileen O'Hara shifted nervously in her chair. 'Are you really suggesting a director—other than the managers—could have been involved?'

Eric shrugged. 'The information I have suggests that Mr Neilson and Mr Daly were undertaking the discussions to contract. There may be an assumption that Mr deSoutier knew of them—and this could be the reason for the management buy-out, with the chance to get hold of a business enterprise that looked set to take off. But maybe he did not know. I think he . . . and anyone else who was involved—or knew of the negotiations—should have the opportunity to wipe the slate clean and declare the interest now.'

Eileen O'Hara took a deep breath. She looked about her. 'Gentlemen . . . this is your chance. Do any of you admit to involvement in these contractual negotiations?' Neilson and Daly seemed puzzled, but she ignored them. 'Or *knew* of the negotiations?'

There was no response. She glared at deSoutier, but he was still watching Eric and made no comment one way or the other.

'Are you satisfied, Mr Ward?'

Eric paused deliberately. 'Did *you* know of these negotiations, Miss O'Hara?'

It was as though he had struck her in the face. The half

smile went, and she glared at him. 'I did not. So . . .'

Eric shrugged. 'So no one knew. Then that raises some further, interesting questions. For I believe there was *one* person who probably did know at an early stage just what was going on.'

'On this board?' she asked angrily. 'Who?'

'Not *on* this board,' he corrected her. 'Just *servicing* the board. It seems logical, and obvious that he might have found out.'

'Why?' Andrew Strain asked, with a nervous edge to his voice.

'Because he'd know most of what went on in the company. He was its compliance officer. He needed to know what was going on. He was the company secretary.'

'Fred Wishart,' Eileen O'Hara whispered.

Eric nodded. 'And the first question that then must be asked is—if *he* knew, *who did he tell?*'

2

The interruption provided by the service of coffee was welcome. As the girls moved around the boardroom table they did so in a complete silence: it was as though each member of the board was afraid to speak in case it would amount to some kind of admission. Andrew Strain rose and walked across to the window to stare out, his back to his colleagues. Ted deSoutier sat with fists clenched together, his mouth pressed firmly against his hands, elbows on the table, staring at nothing, but thinking hard.

Hall Davies was frowning, tapping a pencil against the edge of the table and shooting angry glances from time to time in the direction of Neilson and Daly, both of whom seemed to have been drained of strength. Neilson in particular was sweating heavily: he had the feeling he was due for further cross-examination and he was not relishing it.

When the girls completed the service of coffee and had withdrawn, the silence continued. Eileen O'Hara was staring fixedly at Eric, but the expression in her eyes was confused: she had seen him as an ally, but his insistence that she answer the same question as the rest of the board had shaken her. Nevertheless, it was clear he had more to say that was of concern to them all—and Tom Black knew it too.

He leaned forward. 'Eileen . . . perhaps we should carry on?'

She nodded slowly, her eyes still on Eric. 'I think so. And in view of what Mr Ward has just said, I think the board should give him free rein.'

Andrew Strain turned from the window and strode back to his seat. 'I disagree. I don't like the way things are being presented. Mr Ward has no status on this board. If he wishes to give the chairman advice let him do it outside this room. Clearly, we have a great deal to think about, and consider. I think we need to adjourn.'

'What's the matter, Andrew? Getting nervous?' Hall Davies sneered.

'I resent that! What are you insinuating?'

'I'm insinuating nothing,' Hall Davies replied. 'All I know is that Ward is asking some odd questions—and if he knows something, let him spill it out now. To hell with another adjournment!'

Eileen O'Hara glanced swiftly around. 'I don't think you have support, Andrew. So let's continue.' She turned back to Eric. 'So what is it you want to say, Mr Ward?'

Eric shook his head, knowing he had to take the issues step by step. 'I can't say I know a great deal . . . other than certain questions that should be asked. The first one, as I said, is—who did Fred Wishart tell?'

'Need he have told anyone?' Tom Black asked.

'He should have told *someone* on the board—he was its compliance officer, and responsible for ensuring that all correct procedures were followed. But then again, maybe he intended to do so—but didn't have time.'

There was a short silence. Hall Davies frowned. 'You mean, he died before he could place the matter before the board?'

Eric nodded. 'Which makes one wonder about the circumstances of his death.'

A coldness seemed to descend upon the room as the impact of his words struck home. They all stared at him, sitting rigidly around the table, unwilling to accept the import of his statement. Hall Davies sat back slowly, unbelieving; Andrew Strain's lips were grey. As the tension increased with the silence, it was Ted deSoutier who exploded first.

'That's preposterous! It was a mugging . . . a casual, drug-related attack . . . a robbery—'

'He was killed for a *briefcase*.' Eric smiled cynically. 'Would a mugger really think there was anything of value in a briefcase? Unless there was something of importance in there which he knew about. Such as . . . details of contract negotiations . . .'

'That can't be possible,' Neilson snapped, white-faced. 'Papers were kept under strict . . .' His voice died away as Daly grabbed at his arm, warning him, fearful of further revelations.

Eric shrugged. 'Maybe there was nothing in the case. Maybe Wishart was killed simply to stop him telling the board what he knew about the negotiations . . .' Eric paused. 'How did he get to work that morning?'

There was no response for several seconds. Then Tom Black looked up. 'His car was . . . broken down, I seem to remember. He was driven in by deSoutier.'

'But not home again?' Eric asked.

Ted deSoutier's eyes were hard. Slowly he raised his left hand, warningly. 'Now hold on . . . I drove him in, and agreed to take him back to Regent's Park. But I was called away that afternoon . . . I rang him, told him I couldn't take him home.'

'So you knew he'd be travelling home by Underground to Camden Town, and walking to Regent's Park?'

'So did everyone else who was around that day!' deSoutier snapped. 'But what the hell are you driving at anyway? This is the first time anyone's ever suggested there was any connection between Wishart's death and the affairs of Broadlands.' He shook his head angrily. 'The police have never made any suggestion—'

'They took the easy way out . . . the obvious way,' Eric suggested. 'But then, they didn't have all the facts.'

'What facts?' Andrew Strain demanded. 'All I hear is a series of damned suppositions!'

'Well, they certainly didn't know there had been some rather interesting trading in Broadlands stock before Wishart died, and that trading continued after that date, through a consortium that seemed to know there was the chance of significant gains arising in the near future!'

'A consortium! What the hell are you talking about, Ward?' Tom Black said angrily. 'You're running around in circles!'

'Maybe so. But I just know questions, not answers . . . though I can guess at the answers,' Eric replied. 'One further question is . . . was Fred Wishart an uxorious man?'

'He was in love with his wife, if that's what you mean,' Eileen O'Hara snapped impatiently. 'Even if she didn't deserve it!'

'Did he love her enough to confide in her?' Eric asked.

He saw her face change. For a few moments she did not understand the drift of his remark, but then the realization dawned and her mouth tightened. She continued to stare at him, and he knew her mind was racing, as she put together incidents, and words, and suggestions. 'My God . . .' she muttered.

Ted deSoutier was nervous. Things were getting out of control as far as he was concerned. 'What the hell's going on here?'

Eileen O'Hara stared at him, eyes flaring. 'Fred Wishart would have told his wife. I think he *did* tell her. Months after his death . . . just recently . . . she phoned me, hinted she knew things about your bloody buy-out proposal. Now I know what they were! You bastard!'

'Now hold on!'

'You killed that poor little man! You killed Fred Wishart to keep him quiet, to stop him taking the story of the contract negotiations to the board!'

'You're crazy!' Ted deSoutier shouted. A vein throbbed in his neck, and his face was almost purple with rage. 'You can't hang a story like that around my neck!'

Eileen O'Hara was beside herself with anger. She slammed a hand on the table viciously, and the chair crashed over as she stood up, pointing an accusing finger at the Broadlands managing director. 'And you bloody well followed through, too! You *had* to! After Cynthia phoned me, threatening your deals with exposure, you had to kill her too! That was no accidental fall she had—she was pushed!'

Ted deSoutier was quivering with rage. He glared around the boardroom table. 'Do you hear this madwoman? Can you believe what she's saying? She'll do anything to get at me, but this is crazy! I mean, for God's sake, I didn't even know Wishart had discovered about the negotiations! He knew about Neilson and Daly going to Japan, but I never realized he'd guessed what was going on! I certainly couldn't know he'd told his wife! How the hell could I?'

'Cynthia Wishart had a lover,' Eric said quietly.

Eileen O'Hara was still standing. 'You womanizing bastard!' she snarled.

Ted deSoutier snapped back at her fiercely. 'Am I alone in that, for God's sake? Are we just monks on this board?'

She stared at him, calming down. She turned, picked up

her chair, righted it and sat down slowly, trembling. Ted deSoutier too was regaining control, his flush fading.

'Someone slept with Cynthia Wishart before she died,' Eric said. 'I went to see her that evening. She let me in without using her security system because she was expecting someone else. Once I was there, she was keen to get rid of me—and she told me a concocted story, to explain her phone call to O'Hara. She said it was just a way of gaining attention: she had nothing to impart.'

'But why would she do that?' Tom Black asked huskily.

'I think that after Fred Wishart was killed, Cynthia's lover decided to keep a low profile. He'd got what he wanted from her. Further involvement was dangerous. He stayed away from her. She got lonely, anxious, maybe bitter. In the end, she rang O'Hara, hinting at the contract negotiations her husband had told her about—information she'd given to her lover.'

'Which was when I told you to go around there,' O'Hara intervened.

'That's right. But Wishart's killer also got in touch with her. Said he was coming to see her again. Gave her a reason to back off with the information. And after I'd been and gone, he visited her.'

The room was still and silent as they listened to him.

'Her lover was back. And when she was drunk on vodka, sleepy after lovemaking, maybe he forced some whisky down her throat, so that she vomited eventually, and there was the stairwell in the early hours. She was dangerous to him . . . there was a lot at stake . . .'

'What?' Andrew Strain asked.

'Money.'

'Suppositions again?' Strain asked hoarsely, his mouth slack and nervous.

'With some factual information,' Eric replied. 'My supposition is that Fred Wishart confided in his wife about his anxieties regarding the way the managers were keeping the contract negotiations secret. She in turn told her lover. But the chances are he already knew about the negotiations . . . and had been secretly purchasing shares through a consortium, in order to make a financial killing when the time came. But Fred Wishart was about to tell the board —so he had to die. As Cynthia had to die also, when it became clear that she would always be a liability and could expose her lover's position. Just at a time when the market was really responding to the management buy-out proposal, and the value of the shares was rising.'

'You're talking about a member of this board dealing secretly, using inside information,' Eileen O'Hara said.

'That's right.'

Ted deSoutier grimaced. 'That would be thrown up by the Stock Exchange computer.'

'Unless it was covered by a consortium deal, with people unconnected with Broadlands.'

'That could take years to unravel,' Andrew Strain protested. 'Unless you have some way of knowing who set up the consortium.'

'I have,' Eric said shortly.

'How?' Tom Black asked.

'It doesn't matter how,' Eric replied. 'Let's just say I know that one member of the consortium was a wheeler-dealer called Paulson. In his files there's the name of the person who set up the consortium, just prior to Wishart's death.'

Ted deSoutier's head was lowered. There was a harsh sound from Andrew Strain, his breathing tense and laboured. Eric looked at Eileen O'Hara. There was a hint of fear in her eyes, as though she felt she could be touched personally by what he was about to say. 'The name . . .' she said in a strangled tone. 'What . . . who was it?'

'Someone who was in the office the day Fred Wishart announced he was travelling home by Underground.

Someone who was in the Broadlands flat when you, O'Hara, told me of the phone call you'd received, of the suspicions in your mind about the background to the management buy-out. Someone who realized then that Cynthia Wishart was dangerous, that he had to contact Cynthia again, persuade her to change her story, and then shut her up for good.'

Eric saw that O'Hara knew. It was in her eyes, wide, staring in an initial disbelief, changing to certainty.

'Tom Black,' Eric said in the silence.

3

The beck ran frothing, gold and brown across mossy rocks as it tumbled through the cleft in the hillside to their left. Ravens nested there, their springtime call deeper, more inward-sounding than their normal menacing harshness. As Anne and Eric walked over the contorted whinstone to the shoulder of the bluff the valley opened out below them. They stood among the fern belt and looked out over the heather-strewn slopes, tasting the tang of salt in the fresh breeze, leaning against the lichen-ornamented, weather-beaten rocks at their backs.

Anne breathed deeply. 'It's good to get up here.'

'Away from business,' Eric agreed.

'And the loss of a million.'

'Paulson? Will it be as much as that?' Eric queried.

Anne laughed. 'No, not really. The two million settlement and the insurance cover mean we'll come out with a loss, but rather less than I'd dreaded. Besides, Morcomb Estates has done rather well in the stock market recently. I didn't dare tell you, but Eileen O'Hara's decision to sack the managers and run with the new contracts herself with a reconstituted board has sent our profits up. You see, we've actually been holding a significant amount of Broadlands stock!'

Eric groaned. 'I don't want to know that!'

She laughed, linked her arm in his and squeezed. They were silent for a while, enjoying the valley spreading below them, with the distant view of the roofs of Sedleigh Hall. Quietly she said, 'I hear you were approached to join the Broadlands board.'

'That's right.'

'You turned it down.'

For a brief, flashing moment he remembered the touch of a woman's mouth, warm, soft, intriguing.

'I'm too much in the City already. Leonard's backed down now he can't make a conflict of interest issue stick and Martin and Channing is enough City life for me.'

'I see Tom Black was arraigned yesterday. Will they make the charge of murder stick?'

Eric nodded. 'I think so. There'll be circumstantial evidence. A semen check; fingerprints in her flat, almost certainly; probably other evidence to link him with Cynthia Wishart over the last year or so. It's impossible to keep an affair a complete secret. And then there's the whole financial background . . . his involvement in setting up the consortium.'

'Did he *need* the money?'

Eric shrugged. 'I don't know. I think that like many businessmen—Paulson included—he couldn't resist the opportunity. Once he heard of the projected contracts through Cynthia he saw a way of capitalizing upon the knowledge —buying deeply into Broadlands through a consortium which he could hide behind. And once it had started, he couldn't stand losing out through Wishart's conscience, or Cynthia's possessiveness. He had to act; he had to protect his investment, whether he really needed the money or not. It was necessary to him.'

'A necessary dealing,' Anne murmured.

'Something like that.'

'At least, you can't say I was wrong about Charles

Davison. He managed the settlement for Morcomb Estates well enough.'

Eric made no reply.

He had not told her about Davison, nor would he. But that too had been a necessary dealing.

Donald Enderby had not understood.

'I'm surprised you've got into this kind of dirty business, Ward,' he had said.

'I'm just a lawyer, acting for a client,' Eric had replied stiffly. 'And there's no need to go to court. As I see it, the issues are clear-cut. My client, Charles Davison, persuaded yours to part with a hundred and fifty thousand against a promise to achieve a settlement. Paulson wants the money back—together with an accounting for profits. I can't see either man wants to go to court.'

'Paulson's been defrauded.'

'And even a fraud has rights,' Eric agreed. 'OK. But let me make this admission to you: there are more than enough precedents for us to know any court in the land would agree that the "commission" of one hundred and fifty thousand was really nothing more than a bribe from Paulson to Davison.'

'That's moot.'

'You don't like the word *bribe*? Who cares? The consequence is the money is recoverable from Davison—as money had and received.'

'You'll be advising Davison of that view?' Enderby asked suspiciously.

'I will. He wouldn't stand a chance in court.'

Donald Enderby considered the matter for a few minutes. 'All right. But what about the profits earned?'

'In that issue, *your* client won't stand a chance in court.'

'Why?'

'Come on! The relationship between Paulson and Davison was creditor and debtor. It certainly could not be seen as trustee and beneficiary ... in which case there can be no question that the bribe could be treated as a trust. And so, Paulson can't be entitled to the profits earned.'

'There's a whisper Davison made a considerable amount in an investment with that money—'

'Forget it. Paulson can't touch it. Look, I've marked the passages in the relevant cases ... *Phipps and Boardman* ... *Lister and Stubbs* ...'

There had been a short silence. Then Enderby had nodded. 'I'll talk to my client. He won't like it.'

'Neither will mine.'

Enderby gathered up his papers. 'And I'll say again: I don't like this, Ward. You should choose your cases more carefully. We all have reputations to lose.'

But Eric could not tell Anne that, or why he had taken Davison as a client.

On the other hand, there would be another time, when Davison would be in his sights again. It had been a necessary dealing, for Anne's sake, but he could stand beside her now, in the sunshine, and enjoy the sweep of the Northumberland hills and savour the possibility that one day, in the future, he and Charles Davison would cross swords again.